New and Selected Stories

First Edition

Art on cover © Tania Franco Klein
Proceed to the Route, 2018
Used by kind permission of the artist

The publisher wishes to thank Precious Musa & Cora Lewis.

Library of Congress Cataloging-in-Publication Data
Names: Rivera Garza, Cristina, 1964– author, translator. | Booker, Sarah, translator. | González-Arias, Francisca, translator. | Dillman, Lisa, translator. | Ross, Alex, translator.
Title: New and selected stories / Cristina Rivera Garza; translated by Sarah Booker; with additional translations by Francisca González Arias, Lisa Dillman, Cristina Rivera Garza & Alex Ross.
Description: St. Louis, MO: Dorothy, a publishing project, [2022]
Identifiers: LCCN 2021038245 (print) | LCCN 2021038246 (ebook) | ISBN 9781948980098 (paperback; acid-free paper) | ISBN 9781948980104 (ebook)
Subjects: LCSH: Rivera Garza, Cristina, 1964– —Translations into English. | LCGFT: Short stories.
Classification: LCC PQ7298.28.I8982 N49 2022 (print) | LCC PQ7298.28.I8982 (ebook) | DDC 863/.64—dc23
LC record available at https://lccn.loc.gov/2021038245
LC ebook record available at https://lccn.loc.gov/2021038246

ISBN: 978-1-948980-09-8

Design and composition by Danielle Dutton
Printed on permanent, durable, acid-free recycled paper in the United States of America

Dorothy, a publishing project books are distributed to the trade by New York Review Books

Dorothy, a publishing project | St. Louis, MO
DOROTHYPROJECT.COM

New and Selected Stories
Cristina Rivera Garza

TRANSLATED BY SARAH BOOKER

WITH ADDITIONAL TRANSLATIONS BY FRANCISCA GONZÁLEZ ARIAS,
LISA DILLMAN, CRISTINA RIVERA GARZA & ALEX ROSS

DOROTHY, A PUBLISHING PROJECT

Contents

Introduction

Ricardo Piglia, the Argentinean novelist and essayist, famously claimed that a short story always tells two stories. The two are intertwined, nested into each other's interstices. "A visible story hides a secret tale," he writes. "The enigma is nothing other than a story which is told in an enigmatic way." Nothing more; nothing less. The short story is the name we have chosen to describe the production of the cultural and social space in which something hidden becomes visible, and therefore shared, but still as a secret.

I have reflected on Piglia's provocations quite a bit over the years. At the very least, they have helped me read and revise and re-arrange the stories compiled in this volume. To be sure, Piglia had not published his "Theses on the Short Story" back when I was writing *La Guerra no importa* in the mid-1980s, and I was much too young, much too eager to type on my old Lettera 33, to pause and consider the possibility that "the secret was the key to the form of the story." Yet in my own way, as I strove to get my bearings in a sprawling city in the throes of economic disaster and authoritarian rule, I was thinking of nothing else. The short story allowed me to approach matters that were unintelligible to me—and that's why I felt strangely attracted to them—without betraying their depth and complexity, even their improbability. Approach is the right term here. I saw myself less as someone who explored an issue, and more as the person who, hesitantly, in partial darkness, grew physically and emotionally closer to matters otherwise deadly or dangerous. I never felt compelled, I have to admit, to unveil a secret or deliver a message, essentially because I seldom came out of a short story feeling I had a complete, or even a more thorough, understanding of what just happened. Instead, after every ending I was nagged by the uncanny sensation that I had been close to something I could never fully grasp. That was enough, I told myself; even more than enough. I am still convinced that the slightest attempt at reducing that necessary distance would be literally fatal.

There is much time in these pages, and yet I am still able to make out the young writer I was when first drafting the scenes in which a drifter faces a mirror in a bleak hotel room and calls herself by a name that is not hers, a name that yet another nameless character has bestowed upon her. Greeting herself as another for the first time, that's what she did—and, come to think of it, that's perhaps what I was doing as a writer. The opposite of knowing oneself. Unknowing, that would be an appropriate term to describe both the intimate operation at the heart of the stories in *La Guerra no importa*, and what I thought writing was for. While they were short stories, and thus autonomous units on their own, I conceived of the tales comprising that book as links in a larger arc whose gravitational center was Mexico City as experienced by working class young women yearning for freedom. I thought of *La Guerra no importa* as a novel of sorts: tense, loosely interconnected, always about to unravel. Xian, as the main character is newly named, was a slacker and an occasional thief and a queer liar. Untamed she was in any case, perpetually on the run. Her energy, her slippery ways, her ability to survive, haunted me for a long time. In many ways, I believe I write in order to keep on approaching Xian, even today.

News on femicides and other forms of violence against women came into full view by the end of the 20th century. But a tragedy of this proportion does not grow suddenly overnight. I became a writer in a city keen on closing its eyes before the manifold expressions of the violence that thwarted so many women's lives. I lacked, as did many others, the language to identify and denounce these operations. Yet, I was sure we were in the midst of a rabidly lethal war—a war I thought we had lost from the start. The short stories included in my second collection, *Ningún reloj cuenta esto*, which translates into English as *No Clock Counts This*, helped me approach the relationships between men and women as the gender trouble grew clearer and I found myself decrying love as the main artificer of this conflict. Rather than using the female point of view, I strove to inspect the world that I lived in through men's eyes. I did not want to be a man, but I did want what they enjoyed: unabashed freedom, a voice they never had to justify, the attention they commanded. I hesitated about the title, using a quite benign *Fragile Men* for a while, and toying at times with the more explicit *The End of Heterosexuality*. In the end, I opted for a verse of "September," a poem by Ted Hughes—indeed, *that* Hughes, husband to suicidal poet Sylvia Plath and partner to suicidal Assia Wevill. Unlike mechanical clocks, short stories could count this: the damage, the dilemmas, the asphyxia, the rebellions, the dying.

Migration, which runs in my DNA, has become the most defining feature of my writing life. I came to the United States in 1988, not knowing I was to build a home in this country, not knowing I was to write all of my books from within English but in Spanish. *La frontera más distante,* the title of my third collection of short stories, which translates into English as *The Utmost Border*, is a fragment of a longer verse: The Lotus Tree of the Utmost Border, which according to the Arabic mystical alphabet has two gates: the eastern gate is called Gate of the Appearance of Lights, through which every day 18,000 angels enter. The western gate is the Gate of the Occultation of Light through which these angels disappear, not to return until the day of resurrection. Eschewing realism, places and characters in these stories bear no recognizable human or social names, identifying themselves by fleeting features or the activities they engage with at specific points in space and time. The Woman Who Vanished Behind a Whirlwind. The Man of the Natural Smile. A Snowy Place. Some of these stories find their ultimate home in what Todorov called the fantastic: a suspension of belief, a sudden break with the rules of the real that trigger hesitation in both characters and readers. Some of these stories worked closely with the parameters of the detective story, albeit quite freely. Some others may be best understood through the lenses of what Mark Fisher called the eerie and the weird, which are deeply related to the outside and the unknown. Relational identities as well as secrets abound in these tales—and no one, least of all myself, should dare to unlock the mystery. Instead, do as I do and walk into them, experience the rarified air, look into their vanishing horizon, listen to the beating heart that keeps them on the go. Everything can be something else at every turn. Writing is just a matter of attention; reading too.

In *Diminutus*, a collection of speculative stories and flash fiction that has not yet appeared in Spanish, I have been building small habitats for certain configurations of language. They are short pieces—both because of their dimensions and because of their character as places where something resides. I still think of the word *pieces* as dwelling spaces, which is one of its definitions in Spanish. If a novel is a house, a short story is a piece—*una pieza*—a room, a habitation, perhaps an ecosystem. Only small *pieces* have been admitted, quite fittingly, in *Diminutus*. Far away geographies, languages about to die, gruesome murders, or unleashed wildfires have helped me speculate about endings: the end of our time on earth, the disorienting end of affection, the end of trust, the end of the end. Is it really necessary to live so long, wonders a lonely old woman in one of these *piezas*. I guess I write these stories to approach those kinds of questions.

Reading and revising old pieces is quite an uncomfortable journey. Had it not been for Danielle Dutton and Martin Riker's wild suggestion, I would have never gone back to stories I had either forgotten or had kept on re-writing again and again, mostly unbeknownst to myself. I worked very closely with accomplice and translator extraordinaire Sarah Booker—at times revising her renditions into English, and at times letting her revise my own. I re-wrote more or less at will as I was re-reading the translations, adding and subtracting paragraphs, scenes, or characters where I saw fit. It wouldn't be outlandish at all to say that, based on the collaborative work that went into the process of selecting, translating, and re-arranging, most of these stories are, in fact, quite new. They all remain, however, inextricably linked to novels and poems and even essays I have been developing over time. I am under the impression that I have often written short stories to approach matters I cannot begin to even fathom in larger works. The form of the short story has offered me the economy of devices, the reduction of scale, and the concentration required to dive into obscure matters. The short story, Piglia was right, harbors a secret—and in this secret we will find the key to its form. As the short story artificially makes this secret appear without betraying it, we writers and readers become unsuspecting accomplices, co-conspirators of sorts. We might never agree about the final nature of this secret, but as soon as we look into each other's eyes we will immediately know—and will know it for sure—that we have shared the unintelligible together. We are kin now. We will never be alone.

CRISTINA RIVERA GARZA, 2021

New and Selected Stories

Yoko Ono's Yes

There are several things I will place here: a luminous swimming pool, for example. Look. It is a large turquoise pool in a spa built in 1930, close to a coast. I have the poster that proves it. Here is a spiral staircase made of iron: sinuous and narrow, yes. Rickety. Clangy. The upper landing leads to a window. On the other side of the window is Yoko Ono at the top of the spiral staircase holding the word Yes in her right hand and a magnifying glass in her left.

"It's so you can see better," says the magnifying glass without anyone asking it anything.

This is how we learn that it is not a loupe but a loop. Somewhere in this scene there is a vine. We do not see it, that's true, but we can breathe in its aroma. Chlorophyll is sometimes like that.

Under the spiral staircase, there are stone steps. Made of old rocks. Graphite or malachite, it doesn't matter. A monumental thing. The great leap. Under the stones lies a tiny theater. Within the theater, right on the stage, I will place a man with suspenders and a panama hat and a little dancer with a tulle dress and a diadem of insects.

Look at them.

This is the moment the lights come on. There are whispers. Someone coughs.

"Inhabitants of the summer house," a voice announces.

"Ex-dwellers of the autumn wilds and the winter wilds and the spring wilds," continues the same voice: deep, clean, masculine.

"Ex-wilderners," he seems to repeat, though in reality he says it for the first time.

The lights have changed color and intensity. There are whispers still rippling through the crowd. Someone still coughs. Is that a fly flying? It is a fly, yes, and it flies.

"Inhabitants of the nineteenth century and of the twenty-first century," the echo continues through various speakers.

"Men and women capable of speaking in complete sentences and dependent clauses and freight trains full of accents," he continues.

"Dear astronauts tied to floating objects who stare unblinkingly at a dragonfly while they imagine a cave," he continues.

"All those called Body of Licorice and Mint Tea," he continues.

Now another thing to know: we are on the edge of the luminous pool, under a spiral staircase that leads to a window through which it is possible to see Yoko Ono's Yes. And we are, at the same time, under a stone staircase on which, according to calculations, hundreds of millions of very old shoes have trod to witness, which is another way of saying *to share in*, a little theater piece.

"Inhabitants of the summer," and here the voice raises his voice, "every conversation is a drama, this is well known. Or a comedy."

"Ex-wilderners, inhabitants of the nineteenth century with two knees and a space suit, look:"

(and right here I will make appear the sound of an oar or of several oars on the calm waters of something—I have not yet decided whether it is a river or a lake or one of the four oceans)

This is the moment when the little dancer spins across the stage, over and over again, and again and again with her short tulle dress and her diadem. Her arms held high. Her legs, determined. This is an arabesque, yes. And this is a cartwheel. All the insects are dead. The movement continues without any changes until exhausted, sweaty (the air, in fact, has stopped smelling of chlorophyll to smell instead of sweat, a caustic aroma that enters through the nostril and then drives into the bones), she leans on the heels of the shiny patent-leather shoes of the man wearing suspenders and a panama hat who has watched the whole scene carefully, as she becomes aware of what she has written with her legs along her path:

LET EVERYONE IN THE CITY THINK ABOUT THE WORD YES FOR AT LEAST THIRTY MINUTES AT THE SAME TIME. DO IT FREQUENTLY.

This is the moment when I make them raise their arms and bend their elbows and slap one palm against the other. Now they look at each other, entranced. Now they say, though really they whisper:

the summer has never been so long. This is the moment when she bends slightly forward and touches her lips to the tips of her fingers. See this.

The clear, masculine voice returns through the theater speakers:

"Inhabitants of the stairs and the luminous swimming pools (even those dressed up as ultra-secret agents or Russian farmers or women thirteen-months-pregnant), astronauts who look at the terrestrial landscape with longing, oh so malleable, with atrocious melancholy, all those named Body of Steam from Boiling Water, this is indeed an instruction."

And this is when the lights go out and a red velvet curtain falls with a heavy noise over the stage. Now a helicopter tosses pamphlets out over a graphite city that has been deserted for at least 121 years. The pamphlets contain the word: BREATHE. The words: THIS IS A HUG. Is that a taiga forest? All right, that which can be observed from afar is a taiga forest. Is there someone on the edge of the ten-meter platform who, immobile, with their arms extended upwards, observes the waters that glitter down below? Yes, certainly, someone is there, static. The waters do indeed glitter. There are six kinds of dives: forward, backward, inward, reverse, twisting, arm stand. Judges evaluate six aspects to grade the dive: approach, takeoff, elevation, execution, entry, difficulty. Someone says: but every dive is a dive over an abyss.

Right in this instant I will make the sky tell the truth.

Now is when I smile.

And someone coughs. Yet again. Yes.

PART I

LA GUERRA NO IMPORTA
(1991)

Unknowing

The first thing that woman told me was that she was waiting for her man. Not her husband, not her companion or friend, but her man. They had made a date for six that evening and, after waiting for two hours, she was still hoping he would show. I didn't actually ask her anything; I made the mistake of asking for a match to light my cigarette and, while rummaging in a white handbag full of junk, she started telling me her *marvelous story*, as she called it.

"The only one of my stories full of miracles," she said, "like everyone else's. The same old love story, you know?"

They'd known each other for a little less than a year and had dedicated that time to perfecting the old rituals of touching each other, looking at each other, feeling each other, making each other tremble. The park bench where we were chatting was their meeting place. They usually walked to the closest hotel without saying much.

"What's the point of words in these situations?" Her logic left me speechless. I focused on smoking and looking at the clouds and listening to her as if I was listening to the passage of time. I had absolutely nothing to do and the story of the woman from the park softened the hours, like rain you can smell from far away. I thought she was either an idiot or a madwoman and didn't really give it much thought. When the first drops fell, timid and gooey, she decided she'd waited long enough. In the same distracted and easy way she'd started talking to me, she invited me to get a few drinks. We took off running.

"You know, it's a pity he didn't see me today," she said with words interrupted by panting. "I've never been so beautiful. Look."

She stopped without warning under the rain to show me her lipstick, her silky curls, and, lifting up her skirt with giant purple flowers, she showed me her legs and stockings.

"They're new. They don't have any runs; can you believe it?" Frozen like marble about to become skin or vice versa, her legs looked like they'd been orphaned. "I so would have liked for him to notice that as he touched my thigh," she said, her eyes glued to her own knees.

"It's a real pity," was my only response, and I pulled her by the arm to keep running.

The bar was actually a hole in the wall in a corner of the city, a place with low ceilings and intermittent whispers. I didn't notice the name and barely saw anything because as soon as we sat down the woman ordered two Manhattans.

"Don't worry," she assured me, "I have enough money. Anyway, see the bartender? He was my lover a while ago. A good man," the silence frightened away her words for a moment and then, after a few long precarious minutes, she continued. "In reality he was quite square, full of perfect opinions about every single thing in the world; anyone would've gotten bored with him like I did. No one would put up with him for more than two months, not even you, who seem so patient and sensible." Her comment made me laugh with mixed pleasure and surprise and, like that, with my mouth still open, we toasted. The cherry stem dancing at the bottom of the glass was an enigma, the lost stroke of an overly complicated calligraphy.

I watched her face through the smoke of my cigarette as she downed the first drink like it was water. I was impressed by her fine long nose, the pointed nose of a liar. It was an aristocratic or foreign nose, nothing like the flat or straight noses that abound in the city. I was impressed by her smooth cheeks speckled with freckles, her plump lips coated in nude lipstick, pink like coral. I was impressed by her sparkling eyes. So still, so trustful. The eyes of someone with enough money to drink as much as their body can stand.

"Mauricio, please," she asked the bartender, as if speaking to an old friend, or a personal assistant, for another round of the same. He didn't need to be told twice; he turned around and soon returned with two glasses. She brought the first sip to her lips, then started speaking with a thinly disguised sarcasm, the feigned formality of someone willing to answer a questionnaire.

"My name is Angeles and I'm one of *them*," she said between laughs, really making fun of us both. "Sometimes he stops here, you'll see. This is his favorite place. Mine too. We usually sit at the end of the bar, you know. He likes touching my legs under the counter and he can't do that here, in front of everyone, can he?" Angeles accompanied her words with tiny, timid gestures. Her whole being was revealed in flushed smiles, as if she were a little girl confessing her first acts of mischief to the family priest.

I came to know him, her man, almost completely during the fourth Manhattan: his way of walking as if over clouds, his distractions, the happy days when he shaved a stubborn beard, his tantrums, the exact curvature of his hands sliding across Angeles's back, the coarse hair that swayed over his body like tiny boats in the calmest of seas. Her man.

None of that mattered to me. I've always been skeptical of those sickly emotions that plague women, those epidemics of intimacy and violence that can unfurl in a woman's body as if she's been injected with a deadly virus, an erratic illness that attacks good sense and peace and can transform a beautiful creature into a pile of haggard flesh, expectant, desiring only desire. Something worse than heroin, though no one warns you. Despite it all, I listened to her without any hint of annoyance. The liquor was really too delicious to pass up. And it was still raining outside. And she was very beautiful.

Angeles asked me to light her a cigarette, but it was Mauricio, the bartender who'd been her lover, who solicitously responded. Regardless, she thanked me.

"He's what I call a good man," she murmured, the words crawling one after the other like snails on wet earth. Then she started to cry, not with wild gesticulation, not desperately; she simply let one or two tears roll down her cheeks while she repeated "that's a good man," "that's a good man," like a mantra. As her eyes reddened, I didn't feel intrigued but rather annoyed at still being there, listening to all that nonsense in a story that was proving long and bitter. Angeles was using the whiskey to blackmail me; Angeles cultivated an air of ancient sadness to keep me at her side; Angeles had that look, that mysterious mix of honesty and cynicism unique to distant unreachable creatures, intended to unsettle and attract me. My rage increased every time I realized what I'd gotten into. The total lack of certainty made my hair bristle. Yet she seemed at ease in the uncertainty; she provoked it, received it with open arms like a sacred blessing.

"Come on, Angeles. It isn't that bad, woman," I told her without thinking while I took her hands, and her soft skin, almost invisible, left a strange burning on my fingers. She smiled again, called Mauricio again to ask him for another glass of the same.

"You're right, Xian," she said without worrying whether or not that was my name, baptizing me with all her power. "It isn't that bad, but sometimes, you know, one can be so stupid. He'll come another day. Look, nothing bad's happened here. I'm going to toast having met you."

Then she smiled as if at a dark joke, a tremendous joke. We toasted many times to our meeting in the park and to the rain that had pushed us to her favorite bar and to her impeccable stockings and to the love created by everything and destroyed by everything, to the magical veil with which love covers our faces so that we may better bear the world. Once empty, the glasses clinked together like accidents, cracked crystal.

"That man loves me, Xian, he loves me so much." I never learned who she was talking about, but Angeles, without a doubt, was making fun of herself. Such a snarky woman. She invented a sarcasm very similar to sadness that wasn't sadness but self-pity. She called Mauricio again, but this time she gave him enough money for an entire bottle. And then we left with it hidden under a jacket.

There were few people on the street and thousands of electric moons emerging, yellow, in every puddle. We heard only the echoes of our steps; they sounded so alone. Several times I splashed Angeles's immaculate stockings with dirty water. We were drunk when we wrapped our arms around each other to keep walking.

"Do you remember that song about a hotel for broken hearts?"

I nodded.

"Well, you're going to visit it now. You're going to enter the place where hearts are left all alone and break and scatter like sand. Have you seen your blood?" she cut herself off, looking for another image. "It's like when a window breaks, the glass shreds your bare feet, but you're very happy to no longer have to open it for fresh air. Do you get it?"

I let her talk as we approached a stone building with long windows and wrought iron balconies. When we pushed open the heavy wooden door and crossed the narrow hallway, barely lit by the turbid light of a pair of brown lamps, I understood we were entering another century. Yet Angeles acted like a libertine from ours. With a firm voice, she asked for a room, then indiscreetly pulled out the bottle and placed it on the counter. The attendant looked at us, astonished, uneasy. She hesitated in giving us the keys, yet Angeles skillfully snatched them before she had time to react. Once in the room, its walls briny and furniture rickety, Angeles spent a long time, almost half the whiskey, giving me details and more details about him: his powerful logic; his agile legs, the most agile in the world she corrected herself; his books; his reclusive, skittish bear eyes; the whiteness of his teeth. Listening to her, I thought: this is what it means to latch yourself to another, to be sustained entirely by another. Every time Angeles started in on one of her memories of him, her man, I rushed to take another gulp of liquor because I couldn't stand a woman suffering that way. I didn't know if the nausea came from her repetitive circling of ghosts or the excess of alcohol, but I stood up from the bed and went to vomit in the bathroom. Everything came out, not just the contents of my stomach but also the pain of Angeles's words. Now empty, I went to the sink to wipe my mouth and say goodnight to my reflected image. *Come on, girl, you have to get away from all this, that woman is crazy, Xian, get out of here, you are only human, Xian.* Reminded of my new name, I smiled. I decided I liked being a stranger who talks to herself in front of a mirror in which so many other strangers have surely talked to themselves. Freed of identity, I returned to the space Angeles occupied. I was afraid for her.

"You aren't used to it, are you? Come on, Xian. It isn't that bad, girl," she echoed my words, and I couldn't help but recognize a new jab, a distant hint of sarcasm. "I know I bore you, but it's all over. I'm going to behave. Do you believe me?"

I lay down at her side, thinking about how Angeles had that damned habit of finishing every sentence with a question I never had the answer for. Did I really believe her? She hugged me, and, putting all my weight on her, I felt protected by the humid air that slipped in through the broken windows. I felt protected by the many days and many more years I held within my body. I felt protected from the cold, from the heat. I felt.

"Love is this, Xian, contriving lies and deeply believing them."

I opened my eyes and stared at her nose. It was that. Of course it was that. Pinnocchia. I harbored no doubts then.

Angeles woke me up before dawn. She was getting naked in the most scandalous of silences. She had already placed her flowered skirt on the back of the chair and was delicately rolling down the silk stockings she had stolen from a corner store. I waited while she took off her bra, I waited while she wove her hair into a delicate braid, I waited the whole time because I needed her lap to be able to sleep. Once naked, she stretched out at my side. Her white body between the sheets was the synthesis of something beautiful, something rare, something whose beauty is terrible because it's abandoned and in reach, yet untouchable. No one can touch a madwoman who suffers and makes fun of herself and gets naked. We slept in this embrace until the sun filled the room and our sweaty bodies with shame. We had to get up.

Surely we were both famished, but in her face there was a sort of deep contained violence that filled me with fright. It was the face a captive animal in a zoo makes when a mother brings her child close, showing off the superiority of their species. *Have you seen how beautiful the panther is?* Angeles's lips contracted in a fine tremor, like fury and mockery together. Her whole being appeared in the morning like a weak knot, full of spasms, about to come loose.

We didn't eat anything. We went directly to the park where we'd met and there we flopped down on the grass. We watched pigeons alighting on statues. We watched children running and mothers running after the children. We looked at the sun and it hurt our eyes. Angeles ripped her stockings trying to get close to me. I slept again for a little bit, leaning against her. Angeles didn't sleep; she didn't seem to need any more sleep; it seemed like she was an open-eyed dream. Awake, Angeles seemed to need only alcohol and her man to keep her alive. Surely she was an idiot or a madwoman or both, and I was with her.

I had talked little, it's true. It was also true that I didn't have anything to say. Perhaps that was the reason I began whispering to her in the most moronic soft tones, *everything is stupid, Angeles, so stupid that it isn't worth it.* Angeles stood up, went to throw the empty bottle in a trashcan, and did not return to sit with me.

"Yes, Xian, but I'm going to outwit it all. I'm going to laugh at everything," she shouted from far away, smiling and shaking one hand in the air.

Still on the ground, now leaning against a tree trunk wet from the previous day's rain, I watched Angeles's fleeting ghost. I thought at any moment she might fly off, carried by a pair of enormous white wings: that was when I understood that we had talked about death.

I saw her wave to someone, then, and she kissed him, and they walked, arms around one another, toward the bar. It was six in the evening and he was, without a doubt, her man.

Like Bitches, Like She-Devils

The impossibility of halting the ceaseless flight, the infinite evasion of the Other: such is love's exclusive domain.
ALAIN FINKIELKRAUT, TR. KEVIN O'NEILL AND DAVID SUCHOFF

The kidnapping took place one Sunday afternoon. Xian had been wandering aimlessly for a couple of hours when a man wearing a dark suit and silver cufflinks took her by the elbow and pressed her into a black Lincoln. Under the rain, surrounded by bustling people and untethered noises, Xian looked around and didn't struggle. Once inside the car, the man's velvety voice, the smell of wet denim, and Xian's own empty stomach produced an absurd listlessness, a sort of vertigo.

"Where is she?" the man asked, adjusting his tie. The driver moved through the city's traffic at a normal speed.

"Who?" Xian evaded his question.

"Her," he said, pointing at a photo in which appeared the smiling faces of two emaciated girls.

"Ah," she sighed, as if she had just understood. "Her."

Terri, for the love of god, shut up.

The first name she gave to Julia was Terri, mostly because the woman was, honestly put, terrible, and because her original name

25

was dull, the direct opposite of her personality. They met right at the beginning of the rainy season. Terri waited in the bus line, totally motionless, an umbrella in her left hand, a silk handkerchief covering her orange hair, black boots. Xian concocted the lie when she saw Terri's amber eyes on a coin shining in a puddle. The look of fascination attracted her.

"Help me, some guys are chasing me," Xian said, alarmed but keeping her voice lowered. "Please," she insisted.

Terri turned her face slightly and immediately grabbed Xian's hand and took off running. They crossed dirty streets, whipped around corners, and ran until Xian couldn't anymore and asked to stop.

"Did you know them?" she asked with a sincere curiosity, even with a bit of concern, as they rested in the narrow vestibule of an apartment building.

"No," Xian answered, holding her gaze, unfaltering. She accepted a menthol cigarette. They sat down on a step and watched the drips of the evening drizzle. Soon the rustling of the city enveloped them, and they remained in silence, elbow to elbow, quite at ease. A black dog approached and lay down between their feet. Terri absentmindedly petted it. The smoke from the cigarettes formed figures of intertwined bodies in the air. It was then that Xian burst out laughing.

"You believed it all," she said, staring again at Terri and challenging her with a smirk. To her surprise, Terri met her gaze, unflinching, and responded with a similar expression.

"Truth isn't what's important in this world. Complicity is," she asserted with what seemed like practiced words. "Give me a name, call me what you want," she told her after removing her headscarf, extending her hand.

"Terri," Xian said. The name made them both laugh. Echoes of rain.

The driver took the car to an underground garage. From there, the man led her down dark hallways to an abnormally white room. As soon as he left, Xian settled onto the bed and stared at the cracks in the ceiling. If it hadn't been for her gastritis, she would have fallen asleep immediately. But the burning in her esophagus kept her awake, attentive to all the city noises that filtered through the walls. The color white slowly saturated her senses. A nuclear flower. Her discomfort grew, and, after tossing and turning under the satin sheets, she stood up and went to the bathroom. She took off her clothes in front of the porcelain bathtub and turned on the water. She wanted to rest. She wanted to submerge her face in a warm substance. She did. For a long time. Until she couldn't anymore. And she did it again as soon as she caught her breath. That's how the man found her when he returned for the first time. The face behind the gold-rimmed glasses was expressionless when Xian noisily emerged from the water.

"So you fell in love with her too, you dirty old man?" she said without any warning, half drowning in water and laughter. As his only response, he took her head between his hands and pushed it under. Like before, Xian didn't struggle. Underneath, in the deafening liquid surrounding her, nothing happened. Perhaps that was what death was all about: a befuddled deafness. When she took her head out again, there was no trace of the kidnapper in the room.

Terri, for the love of god, shut up.

They liked sitting on the dilapidated steps of apartment buildings where they didn't live, acting as if the space belonged to them, as if everyone must have previously met them. Sometimes they said goodnight to people; other times they just lowered their gaze while the smoke from cheap cigarettes formed haloes around their heads. Only the dogs approached them.

"She's the devil," Terri said. "A she-devil," she corrected herself.

"How do you know?"

"It's obvious," she said as she held the dog's face in her hands so that Xian could see it better. "She looks like she is looking for an owner, or else for someone to kill."

"Just like you," Xian declared after an uncomfortable silence.

"And like you, my friend," Terri retorted when she let go of the dog's face. "We walk like bitches, we walk like she-devils with this heavy loneliness on our shoulders," she declared. Then she put the final point on it with another loud cackle. And she ran off. The clicking of her black boots got lost in the morning crowd. Echoes on whitewashed walls.

The kidnapper's return was preceded by the bustling of a waiter. The boy placed a folding table in the middle of the room and a

white tablecloth on top of it. Then he brought out silver uten-
sils, white plates, cut crystal glasses, and candles that smelled of
quince. Then he appeared with an order of paella and salads of
cherry-colored fruits. Finally, he placed the champagne in the
fridge.

"Are you hungry?" the kidnapper asked, crossing the door's
threshold, walking stick in hand. "You young people, the only
thing you cannot resist is hunger."

Xian watched him from the bed, completely listless.

"You look good in a white tuxedo," she told him.

"Your little friend lived in my house for a while, did you know
that?" he started telling her as he poured the champagne into two
flutes. "And when she left, a jade collection, a couple diamonds,
and other things of that nature went with her. I don't suppose
you would know where to find it all. Including your wicked little
friend."

Xian kept watching him from afar without the slightest movement.

"You walk like the devil," she told him.

"You were together that whole summer. I know," he was talking and walking and drinking at the same time. "You met in May
and then lived in that sinister building where she rented a room.
You didn't have a job, and she, as far as I know, has never worked
a day in her life. Why might that have been?" he said, a smug
smile. "How is it possible you don't know anything about her, my
dear?"

Xian struggled to get out of the bed and went back to the
bathroom without looking at him. He followed her closely and,

when she turned on the tap and took off her robe, he realized his words were useless. The girl couldn't care less. Defeated, he sat on the lid of the toilet, looking at her sideways. Was she that stupid or just stubborn? Either way, she was not afraid of him.

"That summer we lost six umbrellas," murmured Xian, the water coming up just to her lower lip. "And I lived off the money we made selling your things."

In the discomfort of the silence, the two opted for staring at the ceiling.

"Terri must be in heaven," Xian whispered with her mouth half in and half out of the water. "She must be laughing at us because, you know? Some people die and make fun of us here, all forlorn and helpless. They die because they want to die, or because they've been dead for quite a while and want to catch up. Whatever it is. Whatever happens first," she said, half confessing, half praying for mercy. Or totally out of it.

"Though more often than not people just disappear, you know?" she continued, suddenly looking him in the eye. "They just go away," she added, slapping the surface of the water. "Perhaps they don't want to die after all, perhaps they just don't want to be tied down, you see?" She paused. She submerged herself once again, holding her breath as long as she could. Bubbles. The lungs, heavy. Three more seconds. Thirty. When she came out, gasping violently for air, she wiped the water from her face. "Do you really want to know?" she asked.

"Perhaps they just don't want to hang from the same tree every day, an apple tree, or an immense Christmas tree, it doesn't matter.

The noose around their necks, you see. They don't want that. The noose around their necks as children pull their legs in all that commotion, you know? The cruel commotion of children and the needy," she looked at him, in a trance. "Am I explaining myself?" she finally asked. And she went under the water again, not waiting for an answer.

"When people leave," she said as she came out of the water again, "it means they didn't dare to murder us," she said, as if she had finally had the chance to reveal a long-kept secret. She simpered. She barely shook her head. And in slow motion, she embraced her legs underwater, placing her head on her knees. Her eyes closed. "But if you ask me, dirty old man, if you really want to know, I'd say Terri must be in heaven," she said.

Terri, for the love of god, shut up.

The man stood up in silence and crossed the white room in absolute calm. Before leaving, he picked up the clothing Xian had left on the ground, folded it, and placed it on the bed. The carpet muffled the slow scuff of his solitary steps, but Xian heard the sound of the door handle, the keys landing in the cold paella, and the draft chasing him like a thousand demons around his head.

Behind, under the water, Xian laughed.

PART II

NINGÚN RELOJ CUENTA ESTO
(2002)

Nostalgia

Longing on a large scale is what makes history.
DON DELILLO, UNDERWORLD

The first time he dreamed of the place, he never imagined that, in time, it would become an obsession. After all, it had been one of those light, condensed dreams, the kind that leave you with a pleasant aftertaste when you wake up because you remember every bit of them and then, a few seconds later, forget them just as completely. That morning he opened his eyes and closed them again, stretched, and then, when he was in the bathroom, beneath the cool spray of the shower, recalled everything. He'd been driving an old car, it was white, and he was on a fast-moving road, full of traffic. In the distance, beyond some parched hills, was a cluster of clouds tinged purple and scarlet. Beyond that there was only that sharp yellow light so characteristic of winter. As he sped along he tried to turn on the radio, to pass the time, but after several attempts he realized it didn't work. Then, bored, searching for some sort of distraction, he decided to watch the other motorists. All of them, even the children, were staring straight ahead, toward the end of the road, as if it were salvation, or a prize. But their focus seemed resigned, not hopeful. That explained, most likely, why nobody realized that, as the road got steeper and dusk's colors more intense, an exit came into view. There was no road sign announcing it, nor any indication of its name at the intersection. It was just a little two-lane road with crumbling pavement on which traveled a few other cars as rusty as his own, a bunch of dogs, even a couple of burros. The quadrupeds' presence forced him to slow down and glance constantly in his rear- and side-view mirrors. He didn't want to run anyone over. And proceeding thus, with great care, with uncharacteristic precaution, he realized he was there; this was the place. It wasn't a beautiful place, wasn't even special. In fact, it seemed perfectly at home amid the chaos and ugliness that a lack of city planning had led to. The layout of the streets and range of architectural styles made it clear that no experts had been employed to oversee the urbanization process. You could tell, by the puddles that dogs lapped from and the string of carts parked on one side of the sidewalk, that public ordinances were few and far between and that the police rarely handed out fines. Soon, dusk's shadows made it hard for him to see much more. He turned on his headlights and kept creeping along at the same speed until he pulled to a stop in front of a building with vague colonial influences, with a tiled roof and whitewashed walls. When he pulled on the hand break he realized that before him stood the purpose of his trip. *For rent.* The hand-painted sign offered no further information. When he opened the car door, the outside heat almost forced him to turn back. He did not. Instead, he took off his cashmere sweater, rolled up his shirtsleeves, picked up the briefcase sitting on the passenger's seat and, with a wry smile, thought to himself that those drastic temperature changes only ever occurred in dreams. The possibility of being in one caused him to feel singularly elated, strangely sure of himself.

"I'm here about the apartment," he said to a woman of indeterminate age who barely looked up from the clothes she was scrubbing in a stone washbasin when she heard his voice. The woman made no reply. Silently, she pulled a key from one of the pockets on her blue flowered apron and handed it to him.

"It's on the third floor," she said. "Go on up and have a look."

The staircase was painted red, as were the window and doorframes. The contrast between the red and the almost iridescent whitewash was only slightly diminished by the terracotta floor tiles. Wrought-iron banisters gave an air of reality to a building that otherwise seemed to be there against its will.

"What are you doing here?" a woman with a child in her arms asked the moment he opened the door to apartment 303. Surprised at the woman's presence and disturbed by her empty gaze and the washed-out look of her freckled skin, he didn't know how to respond. Standing stock still, mouth agape, he simply stood there in the doorway without taking his hand from the knob. Once, as a boy, he'd done something similar. He'd stood there motionless, staring at something that surprised him, something he could no longer recall. His stiffness, however, was not caused by fear. Something told him that, if he moved, the moment, that second, would pass.

"That Doña Elvira," the woman finally said. "She always forgets she already rented the apartment and lets all kinds of strangers into my house."

Before she'd even finished the sentence her right hand was pushing one side of the door and unceremoniously closing it on him, forcing him out.

"I didn't mean to . . ." he said, aware of the fact that in some dreams, women with more than four children could never be in good moods.

When he got back down to the building's central patio, Doña Elvira was gone. In her place was a dog, licking the scrubbing stone as if it were his last supper. Hearing the rasping sound of the dog's tongue on the stone and the murmurs of those about to have dinner, he couldn't help but feel grateful that the apartment was already rented. He wouldn't have wanted to live in a building with so much red on display. Besides, he was sure he'd find something better soon. When he got back to his car, he thought about how lucky he was: he'd found the way off the road and could come back whenever he wanted. Then, right before he turned on the engine, he turned to look out at the night. Starlight pierced the dense black sky, and an orange-tinged halo surrounded the pale, round yet blurry moon. The sound of the engine woke him up. He opened and closed his eyes almost simultaneously, stretched, smiled. Then, once in the bathroom, beneath the shower's spray, recalled the dream and realized why he was in a good mood. Later, over the course of the day, he forgot it.

He returned several times, always arriving from a different direction. On his second trip he discovered beanfields bordered with lavender and artichoke. The landscape made him recall the word "bucolic" with a heavy feeling under his tongue. He was driving a compact car, as old as the other one but this time pistachio green. Sporadic buildings and ranches were disappearing behind him. Before him now were dirt roads, zigzagging paths which at that time of day had no one on them. He could tell he was there by the feel of the wind on his face. It was a warmth behind his eyes, a softness in his hands. It was, beyond a shadow of a doubt, a sense of safety. He was pleased to discover that the place was bordered on one side with lush vegetation in a constant state of active growth.

On his third visit he got to see something of the city center. This time he wasn't driving at all, but walking beneath the suffocating midday heat. As he made his way down the sidewalk, trying to take cover in the scant shade cast by the walls, he was unable to recall how he'd gotten there. The dream's invisible hands had taken him to that street and, having deposited him on the pavement, abandoned him with no map in his hands. It took him a little while to get his bearings and a little longer still to recognize the place. In fact, at first he didn't even know it *was* the place. It wasn't until he'd walked up and then down the street that he was sure. Of course that was the place. It was his place, once again. The streets were narrow and the walls were painted bright colors with large ads. There were drycleaners with clean-smelling white steam coming out the doors. The employees, a middle-aged couple with almond-shaped eyes, watched indifferently as he passed by. There were stationer's stores. There were libraries whose shelves were lined with books written in familiar characters but organized on the paper in such a way as to create words he could not recognize. He wanted to flip through one but, just when he almost had it in his hands, an employee asked for his ID. As always, in his dreams, he didn't have his wallet on him. His pockets were empty. With neither hostility nor any hint of kindness, she snatched the book away without explanation. Then she turned her back on him and walked back to her desk, her heels clicking on the floor tiles with telegraphic rhythm. There was also, by the way, a telegraph office in the place, as well as a post office where blue-uniformed men bustled around looking haughty. One out of every five establishments was a restaurant. He walked into the one that looked the cleanest. It was a modest place with an older woman cutting potatoes into little pieces while simultaneously speaking on the phone. When she noticed him, she sent over a gangly boy with big black eyes and a menu.

"What do you recommend?" he asked as he read the names of the dishes. Xianiaqué. Copesuco. Liloduew. Jipo.

"I don't know what you like," the boy answered, shrugging indifferently.

"Almost everything," he replied, trying to be nice.

"So order that," the boy concluded. Then, without even awaiting a response, he dashed out of the restaurant.

The woman brought out a plate piled with ingredients that were unfamiliar and yet gave off tantalizing aromas. He hadn't ordered anything but, since he suddenly realized that he was hungry, he thanked her for the choice.

"The liloduew of the day," she informed him. She extracted a pair of plastic forks from her apron pocket and then simply turned and went to answer another phone call. At first he seriously considered feeding the whole thing to the dog curled up by the door, but his hunger got the better of him. He feared coming down with typhoid or eating feces unknowingly but, squinching his eyes tight, he summoned up his courage. He tried a series of fruits that vaguely resembled potatoes but were purple. Beside them was a pile of vegetables that, on certain parts of his tongue, had the spiciness of arugula, but on others had no taste whatsoever. Everything was covered in a black sauce swimming with little oval seeds. On top of it all, crowning the dish, was a five-petal flower whose pistils resembled sharp teeth. The idea that he might be ingesting a carnivorous flower reminded him that he was in a dream and, just as it had the previous time, this knowledge filled him with a sense of satisfaction and fortitude. Then he devoured everything on his plate and asked for more.

It was after his third journey that he began to sketch one of his first maps of the place. He didn't have much to work with, but little by little, as he recalled details, he was able to sketch a few lines on a piece of white, letter-sized paper. He did it during his lunch break, in his office, with the summer sun on his back. He was sure the place was to the east of a swift-moving road, where the traffic, paradoxically, was always slow. He knew that there were beanfields and seductive smelling flowers growing along one of the borders, maybe the northern one. He knew that the downtown area was bustling with commerce. What he needed, he then realized, was to investigate the west and the south. And he planned to do that on his subsequent journeys.

He wasn't sure if it was on his fourth or his fifth outing that he ended up passing by the building with the tile roof where he'd first wanted to rent an apartment. He looked at it from his car. The whitewash suddenly made him think of the sea, but although he looked around, and then off toward the horizon, he could detect no sign of the ocean. The smell in the air, in fact, was of parched earth, like a valley rising up from the very center of the planet. With that new conviction in his gaze, he turned to glance back at the building. Doña Elvira was still scrubbing clothes in the stone washbasin and the woman with all the kids was running after them, shouting constantly. The central patio which, on his first visit, had had terracotta tiles on the floor, was now gravel. And the laundry lines hanging there had old sheets, overalls, and curtains pinned on them, obstructing his view. The racket made by a rowdy gang of kids running back and forth as if they'd been attacked by a disease with no cure was unbearable. Sooner than he expected, he'd been compelled to start his car and step on the gas with a great sense of urgency. What a relief he'd been unable to rent that apartment, he thought again. In silence, he thanked his lucky stars.

Rather than drift along, this time he wanted to head west. He supposed he'd manage if he just kept turning left, but soon he realized his mistake. That method landed him back downtown, which made him suspect that the streets were somehow organized in a spiral formation. Instead of feeling frustrated, he parked the car behind a cart and began walking. Two blocks later, he almost bumped into the boy with black eyes as he turned a corner. The boy recognized him but didn't stop to say hello. He seemed like he was in a hurry.

"Could you do me a favor?" he asked once he was finally able to catch up with him.

The boy turned to look at him, annoyance plain on his face, and made no reply. He didn't slow his pace, either.

"I want to get to know this place," he began, speaking softly behind the boy's right shoulder, "but I always get lost. Would you like to show me around?" he asked finally, almost out of breath.

The boy stopped, his interest suddenly piqued.

"How much will you pay me?" he asked the man in turn.

He reached into his pants pockets knowing he'd find nothing there but, at the last minute, he fingered the edges of three worn coins. He pulled them out and, one by one, showed them to the boy with great satisfaction. The child snatched them and kept walking swiftly.

"Wait for me," the man shouted when he was about to lose him in the crowd of people on the street. "I want to head west," he informed him.

The boy turned and shot him a scornful look.

"For three coins I can only take you where I'm going," he declared.

He decided that was better than nothing and, having no alternative, followed him.

After crossing wooden bridges over streams full of trash and

turning on corners of what seemed like hilly streets, after passing through a great stone wall that seemed to divide the inside
from the outside, they entered a labyrinth full of people, animals,
and noise. He was sure he'd never been to that area before, and
therefore paid close attention, so that he could add those features
to his evolving map. The boy took him to a plaza with gangly
eucalyptus trees and stooped willows and, once there, abandoned
him. That was the first time he experienced terror in one of his
dreams. He didn't know what he was doing on that bench, watching dogs lick their paws and pigeons take flight the moment the
wind changed direction. He didn't know what sense there was in
continuing to stare at the towers of a church that had no bells.
He didn't know how he'd gotten there and, what's more, didn't
have the slightest clue how to get back out. Besides, the plaza was
full of trash, plastic bags, dog droppings, broken dolls. It wasn't
his kind of place. As soon as the first wave of shock subsided, he
stood and began walking, with absolutely no idea where he was
going. Rather than find his bearings, the longer he walked along
those dirt paths the more lost he got. Soon, probably out of sheer
terror, he lost consciousness. And then he woke up. He opened
and closed his eyes, as always, but this time he didn't get up to go
to the bathroom. Instead of getting out of bed, he curled up under
the sheets as if to protect himself from some metaphysical blow.
The midday sun, later, found him sketching strange lines on a
white sheet of paper.

Days later he decided that indeed that had been the west. The
idea came to him in concise waves when he got back from work.

At first he tried not to think about it, but as the overwhelming sense of horror faded, he dove back into the designing of his map. One afternoon, as he was walking along the seaside in the city where he lived, he saw the sun go down. Immediately he recalled that, when he dreamed about the sunset in the plaza, it had grown slowly, in a rather suspicious manner, before his eyes. And suddenly he had no doubt; certainly, that had been the west. A shiver ran down his spine once he'd fully absorbed the idea. In the future, he thought, he'd take precautions and never, not even by mistake, would he go back to the west. Perhaps it was his own personal version of hell. Perhaps, he thought sorrowfully, there was no heaven in his place.

This new doubt led him to search desperately for the south. And he began to take certain precautions. Before going to sleep he'd drink at least three glasses of water to avoid dehydration and, at the last minute, he decided to slip a compass into the right pocket of his pajamas. Soon he developed a new habit: as soon as he'd get there, he'd take out his compass to orient himself. The people who'd first been surprised by this ritual soon paid him no mind. They probably thought he was some absentminded scientist. He, in turn, refused to be put off by strangers' attention or by the lack of it. Day after day, trip after trip, he made an attempt to find the south. But day after day, trip after trip, he failed in his attempt. The south was elusive. Perhaps the south didn't even exist. That possibility filled him with dread, and dread forced him to slow his outings. And it was thanks to that dread that he finally began to pay attention to the people moving around him.

They were, without a doubt, human beings, not very different in appearance from himself. There were old people and children, all manner of people. Nothing out of the ordinary. When he got close enough, he counted their fingers and toes: five on each hand, five on each foot. Some wore loose clothing that allowed them to move freely; others had on tailored outfits that accentuated the shapes of their bodies. They were enveloped in human smells, too. Sweat, for example. But what he liked most was the way they spoke. They pronounced their vowels like him, broadly. And their tongues fluttered when they trilled their Rs, purring the way he did. More than listen to them, he tasted the rhythm of their words, that nameless melody. As their similarities increased, he saw that his dream was not, after all, so different from reality. And that realization banished his sorrow and brought on a sort of simple, unequivocal excitement very much like happiness. And yet, the one thing he hadn't done was find the south.

On his next trip he left the compass behind and decided to let the stars be his guide. Almost immediately he was able to identify Polaris and, after searching for awhile, he found the Southern Cross. Without delay, he embarked upon a new path with the energy and determination of someone who feels his success near. He hadn't even started to tire when the landscape around him began to change. Instead of the narrow streets and odd houses he was used to, he was now heading into an area that, judging both by its geography and its architecture, had almost nothing in common with the place. There were houses with high roofs that had doves nesting in them. There were avenues with palm trees and daisies growing in the median strips. The uneven sound of syncopated music filled the air with anticipation and excitement. As he wandered contentedly among the steep cobblestone streets and turned corners blanketed in bougainvillea, he realized that many of the large homes had once been movie theaters. In fact, the closer he looked at their facades, the more he could see where the marquees had been. When a gardener who waved his hands generously allowed him to wander around the inside of one of those residences, he ambled blissfully among its lush gardens and the aisles of a theater that was now a family home. The wide-open expanse produced in him a sort of sweet, elusive pleasure, similar to certain women's perfumes. And thus, wandering in and out of houses and alleys, he once more felt that warm tranquility he associated solely with the place. That feeling was the best evidence he had to confirm that, despite appearances to the contrary, this area was not outside or behind, but in the very heart of his place.

Finding the south overwhelmed him with a happiness that lasted quite some time. Colors were sharper and the air less prickly during that period. A renewed self-confidence led him to make rash plans. He'd taste each and every dish in the cleanest restaurant, he told himself. He'd learn the meaning of the words that adorned the spines of the books in the library, he promised. He'd research the place's history and, if it wasn't documented, he'd find a way to do it himself. He'd befriend the natives, start a family. And in time, maybe he'd even change his citizenship. Little by little, as he carried out each of his plans with methodical and serene composure, his face took on the wrinkles of a man who laughs often, the expressions of someone satisfied with his lot. Then, without knowing why, he was troubled by unforeseen concerns. He wanted to go further still. He wanted to discover the great beyond of his place but didn't know how to go about it. The distress he felt at his own uselessness sunk him into a mild depression that, for the most part, he remained unaware of. When he did sense it, though, it was as deep as the roots that kept him grounded in the organic world.

The last time he was in the place, he wasn't really *in it*. He arrived as he sometimes had in previous dreams, via the periphery. He stopped to stare at a wide-open field dotted with white roses, Madagascar jasmine, enormous magnolias. The spot was certainly beautiful, but it wasn't the place he yearned for, the place he'd come to visit. His place. He traversed it as fast as possible, hoping for a miracle at any moment, hoping to blink and find himself on the benches of his own city. He closed his eyes. He opened them. He closed them once more on discovering that he was still there, standing before the field dotted with white flowers. When he opened his eyes once more and saw that nothing had changed, he tried to control his nerves. He walked at a normal pace at first but, when he caught sight of the blue tones of the ocean off in the distance, he knew all was lost. That's when he began to run. He wanted to use up all his energy, to exhaust himself the way those condemned to death did the day before their execution. He went into thirty one-story buildings and, once inside, opened doors to offices whose modern furniture reminded him of his place of work. He rushed out with the same urgency, the same determination he showed every day. Once back on the street, he tried to pick out the fast-moving road that had allowed him to flee the first time. They were all the same; he couldn't find the right one, no matter how he tried. The only one. Then, as he quickly crossed streets and turned corners with the little breath he had left, he glimpsed, off in the distance, the woman with all the kids. She had in her arms, just like the first time, a baby who looked to be only a few months old, but this time there was another child holding her hand as well.

"You lost the way, didn't you?" she asked with an enduring sadness in the hollow passageway of her voice.

He nodded in silence and looked down, ashamed. He didn't know how it had happened. He didn't understand why he'd let it happen. He was so crushed, so lost and disconsolate, that he didn't even notice when the woman disappeared. He tried to find her among the throngs, craning his neck this way and that, but he had no luck. Then, with a torpor that reminded him of something from long ago, he turned and walked all the way back.

"I lost it," he murmured the moment he awoke. "I lost the place."

A woman's face emerged from between the white sheets.

"Rodrigo," she murmured, struggling with the Rs, looking at him out of the corner of her eye. Far from floating in the air like an undulating melody, her voice sounded like breaking glass. It was sharp and clipped, offering no way back. He turned to look at her. He stared with the intensity of those trying to recall something they've lost irretrievably. He was about to speak, to tell her about his loss, but at the last minute he changed his mind. Anyway, the woman had rested her head back down on the pillow and drifted off into a peaceful slumber once more. Her tranquility was so palpable it was almost surreal, as surreal as the majestic view of the Pacific Ocean from his window. The only real thing, the only thing coursing through his body right then, was that nameless void left by the place he'd found and then lost in dreams. The situation was not only grave but ridiculous. And so, in an attempt to recover himself, or to recover from himself, he got out of bed and went to the window. It was Sunday. Whole families wandered amiably down the clean morning streets. The clouds must have arranged to meet on the opposite side of the world, because the dazzling blue sky above was high and perfect. Beneath its canopy, the man began to cry. Then, wiping his tears and his snot, he headed to his study. He opened his desk drawers and took out his collection of imaginary maps. They were stored in a series of notebooks with brown covers. The early ones, the ones he drew when he was just barely getting to know the place, bore the marks of a beginner. It was obvious in the lack of proportion, the hesitant pencil strokes. With time, though, his cartography had improved. The latest ones, in fact, the ones that included the south, looked like they'd been made by professionals in the field. He looked at the dates he'd jotted in the upper right-hand corner of each map. The first was from 1984. The last, from 2000. May. Without thinking, he went back into the bedroom, the wrinkled maps in his hand. He was beside himself. He raced around. With no warning whatsoever, he violently shook the sleeping woman.

"My name is Rodrigo. You hear me?" he shouted almost into her mouth. "R-o-d-r-i-g-o," he repeated, enunciating each letter of his name with incredible earnestness. The sound of his own voice alarmed him. In its slowness, each letter of his name was like a pin under the fingernails of his own language. A form of torture.

The woman immediately stretched and opened her eyes wide. All at once, horror flooded her green pupils. The man left as he had come: with no warning, enraged, out of the blue. Once he was no longer beside her, she set about collecting the wrinkled papers he'd left in his wake. She looked at each of them. She scrutinized them. She made calculations. Gradually it hit her, it was all so obvious, and the realization forced her to close her eyes and cover her face with the pillow. She felt an enormous emptiness in her stomach. She felt like she was going to vomit. In that moment, she finally realized that she'd spent the last sixteen years of her life with an immigrant, a man who, strictly speaking, had spent those same sixteen years someplace else.

TRANSLATED BY LISA DILLMAN

The Day Juan Rulfo Died

I met Blanca at the café downtown at six in the evening, as we had agreed. As usual, she was already there, waiting for me at one of the corner tables far from the windows, the hustle and bustle of the waiters and street vendors. We kissed each other on both cheeks and smiled. A half-smoked cigarette burned from the ashtray and her old black notebook lay open. She said she'd already ordered my espresso.

"I stopped drinking coffee exactly four months ago, Blanca," I told her.

The news didn't surprise her. She was distracted, scrawling a final line on the gridded pages. When she finished, she tossed her fountain pen into a little wooden box and, still not looking at me, laced her fingers together and focused on cracking her knuckles one by one, starting with the pinkies. The sound irritated me, as it always had, but I abstained from making any comment to avoid an inconvenient quarrel. It had been a little more than half a year since we'd last seen each other and more than three since we'd lived together, but for one reason or another we had never lost touch. First it was the prolonged negotiation over the car that she ultimately ended up with, then the exchange of books and albums we had bought as a couple without clearly defining the owner. Later, we started to see each other just to criticize our current lovers. Some were too irresponsible, others very boring, the majority too young and immature, but all of them, without any doubt, stunning. There was no hint of flirtation in our acidic remarks. Blanca and I knew quite well we would never again share a house, much less a life.

"I'm pregnant," she announced with her eyes glued to her drab cup of coffee.

Her straight hair was dry, her fingernails bitten to the quick. I didn't know if I should congratulate her or offer to help her contact a doctor. Blanca had always maintained that she would never have children, but she did so in the same voracious, stubborn way I'd sworn more than once that I'd never give up my espresso. When the waiter approached the table, I asked for a bottle of mineral water and a lot of ice. She kept smoking, a wan smile on her face.

"Can you imagine?" she said.

"No," I immediately answered.

Then I took her hands. The skin on the backs of them were coarse and her palms covered in sweat. Blanca didn't want congratulations.

"What are you going to do?"

"I don't know yet, but suicide is off the table," she joked.

The smile froze on her face. Through her parted, dry lips, I could see her jagged teeth. It was difficult to believe I'd once loved her; that, once upon a time, her wild energy and cackles would have had me hanging from her coattails, docile as a lamb waiting to follow her delirious commands. For two years. How had I once thought I could hold the world just to have the opportunity to give it to her at the mere mention of her name, her full name, Blanca Florencia Madrigal.

"And how are you?" she asked.

I thought about the half-written essay on my desk, the flat tire on my car, and the shapely legs of one of the students who sat in the front row of my class, but I couldn't make up my mind what to mention. I was going to start to tell her about my latest adventure with a girl who shaved her pubic hair, but I didn't know where to start. I tried to outline some images of the most recent changes I'd made in my apartment, but everything seemed so boring. I could describe in full detail the endless hours I spent grading incorrigible exams or discovering new cracks in the white walls of my office, but I knew that would bore her. Without Blanca, my life had become peaceful. I got up early, got to work on time, bathed every day, and had even quit smoking. Without her tumultuous presence at my side, the members of the Philosophy Department had started to take me seriously and, in fewer than three years, I had been promoted twice. It had been a long time since I'd thought about suicide.

"Good," I told her. "Getting on."

Blanca wasn't paying any attention to me whatsoever, but I, secretly satisfied, was comparing her worn face and clumsy movements with my new confidence and autonomy. I no longer belonged to her.

A man with long hair and round rimless glasses approached our table. He caressed her shoulder and kissed her on the lips. He must have been at least ten years younger than either of us and was, without a doubt, much better looking. I assumed this was "the father" and I wasn't wrong. Blanca introduced us, and he pulled up a chair to be close to her. Then he calmly draped his arm across her shoulders: his hand covered in silver rings and leather bracelets hung below her collarbone, almost touching her breast. Seeing him, I couldn't help but think that Blanca must have still been very good in bed, otherwise it would be difficult to explain what this young, seemingly well-educated man, one possibly even sought after in his circle of friends, saw in her.

"Blanca's told me a lot about you," he said with a calm, direct voice.

I frowned and changed the subject. I mentioned some failed strikes, the rampant economic crisis, and the kind of things everyone inevitably agrees on: this country is full of shit. The longer I'd been apart from Blanca Florencia, the more the thought of her had made me uncomfortable. When I agreed to see her, I did so under the condition that we would be alone, and when anyone asked me about her, my usual response was to shrug my shoulders. Why would I know anything about her? During our years together, my fidelity and her constant adultery became almost legend. It was enough for me to make a new friend for Blanca to develop an interest, and he would end up spending the mornings in our house, occupying a place that was mine. The same happened with female friends. I, on the other hand, didn't find anyone interesting enough to cause me to stop giving Blanca my unconditional attention. Her manias, her suicide attempts, her incomparable sexual skills—these consumed all my time and energy. In the end, deciding I was getting old and boring, Blanca brazenly left me for another man. In under two months she exchanged him for another and that one for another, while I opted to return with renewed energy to my studies, less out of sincere interest and more to prove I wasn't getting old. At first, right after the separation, my devoted dedication to writing essays and teaching classes had no other intention than to get her back. I wanted to own the world, the whole world, just to have the opportunity to wrap it up in wrapping paper and place it in her lap. Blanca, however, was never interested in the world. As she got away for good, without any possibility of returning, all that was left for me was my work. I imagined the young man was aware of all that and, downcast, almost ashamed, I avoided further conversation. What could she have told him, anyway?

"Your weekly column is fantastic," he said. "I never miss it."

His curved fingers rested on Blanca's collarbone. My hands were wrapped around the cold glass of sparkling water. I lowered my gaze, wanting to smile condescendingly or at least ironically, but I couldn't. His words, like those of my students, weren't belligerent but innocent. There wasn't any point to fighting. The murmurs of the café distracted me: the sound of spoons clinking against plates and forks falling to the floor had a syncopated, almost happy rhythm. I turned to look at Blanca and, again, I couldn't believe I had once loved her. With their tattered clothes and their faces drained by numerous sleepless nights, the two looked like they were going downhill fast. Enveloped by the gray smoke of the cigarettes, they had the saturnine aura of losers and addicts.

After an uncomfortable silence, Blanca and her friend invited me to the movies.

"We got free tickets," they told me triumphantly.

Their innocence made me laugh. I claimed non-existent obligations and my workload to take a rain check. I paid the bill and extended my hand to them before leaving.

"Congratulations," I told them.

I was certain Blanca would not get an abortion.

Outside, the nighttime January breeze forced me to pull up the collar of my jacket. I wandered aimlessly thinking about Blanca Florencia. The memory of our passionate fights followed by the hours of Olympic sex left me unfazed. It was impossible for me to remember the reasons that once triggered the slaps and shouts, the moans, saliva, and semen. The cold forced me to pick up my pace and, as I crossed streets and turned corners, I noticed I was out of breath. The sensation of asphyxiation became so strong that I had to stop. I leaned against the doorway of a dark apartment building, rubbing my hands together, desperately trying to catch my breath. I tried to forcefully inhale and exhale a couple of times but to no avail. The air became increasingly thin, increasingly scarce. The air passed by me as if I didn't exist, refusing to enter my nose and lungs. I sat down on a step, panting. My knees were shaking. I thought I was about to die, that there was no solution or way out and, in that moment, like a well-sharpened dagger, the violent image of Blanca ripped through the screen of reality. A weak light filtered through the crack from the other side. Captivated by the desire to have her close once more, I lowered my eyelids, closing my eyes.

"Don't worry, everything's ok, you just lost your breath," said a little man with long tangled hair who was holding a shoulder of booze below my nose.

"It happens a lot around here," he added.

With my head still on the concrete, unable to move, I assumed I had fainted, but I had no idea what actually had happened. I slowly sat up, afraid of a second bout. I opened my mouth wide and, after holding the air for a moment, expelled it with pleasure. Everything had gone back to normal.

The little man offered me a swig of the liquor with his trembling, dirty hands. I accepted without thinking twice. The lash of the mezcal at the mouth of my stomach woke me up.

"I've seen many fall like that, but you were lucky," he murmured.

He sat down at my side. As he spoke, a rancid, whitish vapor escaped from his mouth, covering his face entirely. When he fell silent, I realized he was a dwarf. He had a dark birthmark above his upper lip and deep acne scars all over his face. A scraggly beard hung down to his chest. Even though it wasn't all that late, no one was walking on the street. It was the two of us alone, there, the dwarf and philosopher beneath the doorway of a rundown apartment building, in the dark. The mezcal protected me from the cold and fear. I looked him in the eye. He looked at me blankly.

"What did the three wise men bring you?" he asked in a nasal voice.

I hugged my knees, trying to find some warmth in my own body.

"A woman," I told him.

He wrapped himself up in his wool sweater, took another swig from his bottle, and shrugged his shoulders.

"And what happened? Did they take her away?"

"Many years ago," I answered.

The desire to have Blanca physically close again overcame me completely. A mute within me shrugged my shoulders, opened my mouth, made desperate gestures toward the world, and then, defeated, returned to its stony stillness.

"I would have given my life for her," I murmured.

The dwarf passed me the bottle.

"You did," he said.

Blanca Florencia Madrigal. Her name fell in my head with the cadence of drips from a leaky faucet. There she was, in each drop, chasing ladybugs around the trees, guiding my trembling hands over her breasts, standing naked in front of mirrors. I wanted to hang from her shoulders, hide beneath her skirt, breathe in the smell of her hair. The desire grew; the desire to embrace her and not let go; the desire to kiss her thighs, to be once more the teenager in love, stupidly, at the total mercy of a crazed woman; the desire to wander aimlessly on rainy summer afternoons and make love behind the altars of crowded churches; the desire to watch her seduce our friends in common with the slyest gestures and to listen, afterward, to the detailed account; the desire to fall to my knees and plead and beg with all my heart, Blanca.

Suddenly the final scene of our breakup came into my mind. We were lying in the fragrant grass of a park and Blanca had just told me that nothing mattered anymore, not even us.

"But you're my life, Blanca, my whole life," I had told her when I didn't have anything else to say.

Blanca stood up, started spinning on her own axis, her flowered skirt extending like a parachute.

"But life is so meaningless, darling. Haven't you realized?" I had the world there, in my pocket, saved as a gift, and there it stayed.

When I turned to look at the dwarf, nothing seemed strange.

"But life is so meaningless," I told him, looking him in the eye, feeling Blanca's words like needles under my fingernails.

"That's true," he answered coolly.

The dwarf threw the empty bottle into the vacant lot next door. The sound of the glass crashing against the rocks stretched down the black street until, a while later, it disappeared completely. In silence, with difficulty, he stood up. Then he extended one of his chubby hands to help me do the same. He asked if I felt all right and, without waiting for my answer, told me it would be best if I left.

"It's dangerous to walk around here at night," he warned me. "Protect yourself from the pollution. And watch out for the air," he advised as he brought the palms of his hands together and cupped them over his mouth, showing me how to do it.

I had no idea where I was. I walked for hours trying to read the street signs or stumble across some building I recognized, but all in vain. *The murmuring perplexed me. The walls seemed to distill the voices, they seemed to be filtering through the cracks and crumbling mortar.* It had been a long time since I'd been in the heart of Mexico City, the downtown district where I'd lived with Blanca, the historical district that was not mine but hers. That, at least, I hadn't forgotten. *A human voice: not clear, but a secretive voice, like a buzzing in my ears.* Almost at dawn I found myself before the Palace of the Inquisition. I moved quickly through the Santo Domingo Plaza, trying to skirt around the bodies of the street dogs and drunks sprawled on the ground. The silence was now absolute. With the sun still paused somewhere behind the horizon, the sky acquired an exaggerated and violent clarity. Then, almost without transition, it shifted to its usual bluish gray. I was walking slowly, unrushed, trying to overcome the cadence of the morning wind. Meanwhile, the stone mute that lived in me *fell to the ground with a thud and lay there, collapsed like a pile of rocks* before my static eyes until not even a sigh of dry dust was left. I saw Blanca Florencia, watching me, falling to her knees as she played with the clumps of dirt. Her eyes dull, remorseful, needles under my fingernails. I tried to see her, less each time, until her image was *so thin it slipped through my fingers forever.* I mean forever.

With nothing inside, flat and desolate like the esplanade where I walked, I understood with terror each and every one of the reasons I had loved her. Then, almost immediately, I forgot them again. Once in my apartment, I took a hurried shower and brushed my teeth. I arranged a series of papers in my briefcase and, with it in my hand, ran back out to get to my first class on time. I didn't have the slightest idea what I would talk about with my students that day. They greeted me with the news that Juan Rulfo had died. It was January 7, 1986, and I, standing behind the desk, motionless like a statue, looking out the windows, watched how life ran terrified down the streets, all of life; life, which is always so meaningless, which is never enough, Blanca.

Pascal's Last Summer

Teresa Quiñones loved me because I used to watch her in silence as she held forth on the dissolution of the ego.

"And who are you?" she would ask me at the end of her speech.

"Whatever you want me to be," I would answer her, shrugging my shoulders and reflecting her smile, which bathed me in its light. My answer made her happy.

"The world, unfortunately, is real, Pascal," she would then say, pursing her lips in a gesture of resignation. Then, as if her happiness were only a brief interruption, she would continue reading books by dead authors, wrapped in her purple sari, reclining against the large cushions in the living room. Then I would head to the kitchen to grind coffee beans so the cappuccinos would be ready when her sister Genoveva arrived. When Genoveva appeared in the doorway, with her somber-colored skirts and her low-heeled shoes, the house filled up with the scent of gardenias.

"Two lumps of sugar?" I would ask, more to carry out a ritual than to get an answer. Genoveva would smile, joyless, but with complete sincerity.

"You know I don't take sugar, Pascal," she would answer as she hung up her purse and jacket, turning her back to me. Teresa, absorbed in her endless prayers, would drink her cappuccino with her head buried in her books or gazing at the wall without actually seeing anything. Genoveva and I, on the other hand, would take our places at the kitchen table and gaze at each other, which provoked spontaneous smiles from both of us. Unlike Teresa, Genoveva loved me because I always let her remain silent while I related trivial events.

"Yesterday I saw a picture of the fattest man in the world," I told her between sips of coffee. "It was intriguing."

Genoveva would smile kindly, without saying a word. That was the moment when I would take my opportunity to stand behind her and give her a circular massage at the base of her neck. The moans that came from her mouth excited me. But nothing more ever happened because that was when Maura Noches, the Quiñones sisters' best friend, would usually drop by. Her freewheeling chatter and the whirlwind of her arms and legs interrupted Teresa's concentration and Genoveva's circular fatigue. At that point, we would all move to the living room.

"Did any of you see the picture of the fattest man in the world?" she would ask, as if it were a question of life or death.

"As a matter of fact, Pascal was just telling me about that," Genoveva informed her, unintentionally provoking a sudden smile on Maura's face.

"That's what I like about you, Pascal," she would say without blushing at all. "You notice the same things I do," which was actually only half true.

Maura wore her hair short and her pants so tight that it was difficult for her to sit down on the floor next to Teresa. When she finally managed to do so, she crossed her legs with a studied nonchalance that was so well practiced it looked almost natural: the eternal diva. In that pose, she lit her cigarettes dramatically and went on chatting about inane topics that, in her voice of a thousand textures, sounded like enchanted mysteries. Teresa would eventually get bored and go off to her room to continue reading. Meanwhile, Genoveva would make an effort to keep her eyes open and look interested, but after half an hour she too would find a pretext to leave the room. At this point, Maura would take advantage of our time alone to move in closer to me with her seductive gestures and girlish voice.

"Did you notice that somebody stole the mouthpiece from the telephone on the corner again?" she would ask, more to confirm that we both noticed the same things than to find out about the fate of the telephone.

"But that happened three days ago, Maura," I would tell her, and she would immediately pounce on me because my answer validated her theories. Caught up in her turbulence, sometimes we would kiss behind the curtains and at others we would lock ourselves in the bathroom to make love at different speeds and in as many ways as the space permitted.

"What are you going to do with me?" I would ask her in a low voice when she had me under her, vanquished and unresisting. That question always drove her wild.

"You're the perfect man," she would assure me as we both came. After that she would wash herself, get dressed, and, standing in front of the mirror, she would tuck her reddish hair behind her ears. As she applied her chocolate-colored lipstick, she would blow me noisy kisses without turning her head around.

"Intensity is what counts most," she would say, still pure reflection. Looking at her from my position, with the scent of her sex on my hands and mouth, I agreed with her. The world, unfortunately, was real, as Teresa was fond of saying, but that didn't bother Maura, and it didn't bother me either as long as I could continue performing arabesques with her body.

"You and I understand each other very well, Pascal," she would insist. Then she would take her purse and rush out the door in order to avoid running into Samuel, her official boyfriend, or Patricio, her unofficial boyfriend, for both of whom I was neither a man nor perfect, but rather a loyal confidant.

"I don't understand Maura," Samuel would complain. "I give her everything, and she gets it on with everyone else in the neighborhood."

"Maura is incomprehensible," Patricio would moan. "I take care of her, and I do everything to please her, and look how she pays me back."

I would listen to both of them attentively. Samuel was a slender man with straight hair who had probably never done anything illegal in his life. Patricio was a golden-skinned boy who had doubtless been loved by many women. I used to get together with Samuel at an outdoor cafe surrounded by jacarandas, whereas I would see Patricio on the sports fields, where the Sunday soccer players used to congregate. One would ply me with raspberry pastries and the other with ice-cold beers in order to find out some secret that would enable them to dismantle Maura's heart. I didn't understand why they wanted to do that, but when they asked me for advice, I told the first one that you could never give everything to a woman like Maura, and I told the second one that a woman like Maura never *paid*. After listening to my advice just as attentively as I had listened to their grievances, both of them would head home with heavy steps and slumped shoulders, without noticing the cat eating the remains of a fish behind the Chinese restaurant or the new photographs of naked women decorating Chema's garage.

"So, you're screwing Maura now?" the mechanic would ask me, thrusting his hips forward, every time I walked past his garage. "Ya lucky devil," he would say, erupting in riotous laughter. I never understood what he meant by "devil," and I didn't like being called lucky either. I was sixteen, and women loved me; that was all. Luck had little or nothing to do with it.

In those days, I lived on the top floor of a building that was about to collapse, so the damp attic with sky-blue walls that my parents paid for from Ensenada didn't cost much. Every month, I received a money order that allowed me to pay the rent as well as buy a bit of food and an occasional book. The rest I got from the Quiñones sisters, who adored me, or I would get it from the grateful hands of Samuel or Patricio, who gradually became my friends. Nevertheless, my mother worried constantly about what she called my "meager" existence and she expounded on this topic in each and every one of her letters.

Pascal,

I hope this letter finds you in good health and in better spirits. Back home things are pretty much the same or maybe a little worse. Your sister Lourdes has a new boyfriend, a boy named Ramón Zetina, and I'm sure she'll end up marrying him, which doesn't make me very happy because the man has no character, and your sister meddles in his business whenever she feels like it; and you and I both know what happens to families without a man who knows how to take responsibility. The upshot is, I'm very worried that he'll end up like your father, who still would rather count ships passing by the docks than work in a factory eight hours a day in San Diego. So, my dear Pascal, use your time in the capital well to turn yourself into a real man. Nothing would give me greater pride.

Your mother who loves and misses you

For some reason that I never was able to understand, my mother's letters always filled me with sadness. I suppose that's why I read them all as quickly as possible and left them lying, unintentionally, near the wastebasket. Then I would rush to the Quiñoneses' house, which was only two blocks away. On the way, I would buy coffee beans and notice the telephones, the puddles, the pictures at the newsstands, and the voices of street peddlers. When I crossed the front yard, which was dotted with arum lilies, my lungs filled with the scent of roses of Castile and I left the city behind, because in order to enter the world of the Quiñoneses—this had been clear from the beginning—everything else had to be left behind. As soon as I opened the front door, I would already be feeling much better. It was enough for me to see Teresa in her saffron-colored sari and her long braids sprinkled with brilliant little stones, and I would be invaded by a strange feeling of well-being. In this state, I would calmly sit down near Teresa and pretend to read one of her books.

"Identity is an endless flight, Pascal," she would say with astonished eyes and in a grave tone. "We can never defeat reality," she would conclude. I admired the way she tormented herself every day, and so I would lean back in her lap and wait for the flow of her words to wash over me.

"Don't worry, Teresa; I can be whatever you want me to be," I would assure her, with my face close to her breasts.

"I've already told you, Pascal," she would admonish me, "You're empty. Do you know what the word 'vulnerable' means?"

I didn't know, and I saw no point at all in questioning her opinions. I would merely smile at her in perfect calm and total silence. Sometimes, she would place her right arm behind my neck. At other times, if she was in a good mood, we would kiss silently until we heard Genoveva's weary steps approaching the front door.

"Two lumps of sugar?" I would ask her, and she would smile in a way we both understood. Later, Maura would arrive and change everything with her presence.

"Did you see the cat today?"

"Behind the Chinese restaurant."

"And the bullfighting poster?"

"It's been there for two weeks, Maura." The interrogation could last minutes or hours: Everything depended on how long Teresa could last without a book or the constitutional fatigue of Genoveva. Once we were alone, all I had to do was wait. If I had learned anything at all in the many afternoons I'd spent at the Quiñoneses' house, it was that the only way to be with Maura was to wait, and I did just that, with an almost religious faith and dedication. I would wait in the armchair, and she would arrive, inevitably and at her own pace.

"You're my magnet," she would say. And at that moment my eyes reflected the wonder she inspired in herself when she was able to make me her lodestone.

"Fuck me," I would murmur from the tip of my tongue, and Maura would have no other choice but to obey her own desire. Sometimes she would unbutton my shirt on the way to the bathroom; at other times, she would take me by the hand and sing a lullaby on the carpet. Her desires were my desires. I may have been vulnerable, as Teresa contended, but my helplessness and vulnerability transported me to places where I was happy and where I felt contented. The Quiñoneses' large house was one of those places. There, amid the scent of incense and under the slanting light of the late afternoon, all I needed was to abandon myself in order to be what I truly was. I had no desire to change. I didn't want to become anybody else.

The world, unfortunately, was real. Far from the Quiñoneses' house, the world harried me with its demands and its suspicions.

Patricio, for example, spoke less and less about Maura when we got together and more and more about the strangeness of the sisters.

"And you think going around wrapped in those colored rags is normal?" Patricio wondered aloud as he sipped his beer.

"It's an East Indian dress called a sari," I pointed out, repeating Teresa's words. "And besides, it's pretty." He shook his head.

"They're contaminating you with their weirdness, Pascal," he would warn me as he walked away with a frustrated smile on his face. I hadn't begun to doubt yet.

Samuel, for his part, began to worry about my future.

"What are you going to do when you grow up?" he would ask me from time to time, just when I was most enjoying the apple tart and espresso coffee he treated me to regularly.

"But I'm already grown up." My answer only caused him to smile derisively.

"You can't just be the Quiñoneses' sex object for the rest of your life, Pascal," he told me. "That is, of course, unless the only thing you want to be in life is a gigolo."

His choice of words precluded any kind of pleasure I might have felt. Sex object. Gigolo. Grown-up. Sometimes I felt like retorting with one of Teresa's demolishing pronouncements, but when I saw his eyes fixed on mine, I would be invaded by feelings of fear and compassion. What could I possibly say to a man who was incapable of seducing Maura, the easiest of women? Instead of destroying his world, I would let him continue carrying around his conviction. It weighed so heavily on him that he walked with slumped shoulders and downcast eyes, turned inward and oblivious to his surroundings.

Samuel and Patricio moved me to pity and made me doubt, but for several months I continued visiting the Quiñoneses' house in spite of their warnings. As soon as I crossed the gateway into their garden, I felt safe, and once inside, I forgot about any doubts or misgivings. Neither Teresa nor Genoveva nor Maura demanded anything of me, not even that I visit them, and yet when I did drop in, all three enjoyed me as much as I enjoyed them. I thought I was happy. And maybe it was because I was happy, but without being fully conscious of it, that one afternoon I approached Teresa, not with my usual silence, but with an unexpected question.

"You know, Teresa," I murmured, my head close to her breasts, "for a while now, I've been trying to figure out what I'm going to do when I grow up."

"But you're already grown up," she answered, gently pushing me out of her lap and forcing me to look her in the eye. The total surprise in her eyes filled me with a different kind of fear.

"It's the world, isn't it, Pascal?" she murmured softly.

"Unfortunately," I answered, more as an automatic reflex than because I truly felt that way.

Nothing was the same after that. Small gestures of rejection became a common occurrence, at first barely perceptible, but, with time, more and more direct or even brusque. For example, when I would remain silent during Teresa's disquisitions, she would look at me with unwholesome curiosity.

"What are you thinking about, Pascal?" she would ask. None of my answers satisfied her, and she would respond with a silence even more ominous than my own. Later, when I tried to massage Genoveva's tense neck, she would squirm on her chair with impatience and apprehension until finally she leapt up like a skittish cat, and in that moment, the bond between us was permanently severed. As for Maura, she no longer desired my desires, even though I desired hers more than ever. As the rhythm of my routine at the Quiñoneses' house began to alter, I would feel more and more nervous while there. Patricio was right: Teresa's sari might have been pretty, but it was definitely uncomfortable. Genoveva's fatigue had no real justification. Maura was promiscuous. And I—Samuel was right about this—had become the puppet of three lunatic women.

Over time, I began to visit them less and less. Instead of going to their house, I would head for the soccer field where I would meet Patricio, or to trendy restaurants where I would eat thanks to Samuel's generosity. My appearance also changed. I cut my hair and stopped wearing the moccasins that Genoveva liked so much because they made no noise on the floorboards. My button-down shirts were gradually replaced by wrinkled T-shirts with soccer team logos emblazoned across the front.

I started to chew gum and smoke every once in a while. Unwashed and unconcerned about my appearance, I spent most of my time with men. Soon, I began to notice that the main thing we talked about was women. We used all the grammatical tenses: what we were going to do, what we would do, what we would have to do with them. And so, when we were together, with sly, contemptuous leers, we would practice every form of sarcasm.

"Maura is a whore," I said once in a tavern, surrounded by friends. As everyone seemed to be paying attention, I went on to regale them with detailed descriptions of some of our erotic adventures in the Quiñoneses' bathroom. Although the alcohol and the laughter made my head spin, I couldn't help noticing that, perhaps unintentionally, I had edited my story right and left. I never mentioned, for example, that in order to have Maura between my arms and legs, all I had to do was bide my time in the armchair in the living room. When I uttered the words "fuck me," I put them in her mouth and not my own.

According to my tavern tale, Maura would always say that I was the perfect man after we had sex. I never made any mention of her idea about intensity. Thus, deprived of what had made her so irresistible to me, Maura was in reality just a woman like any other. A holy whore. And I resented her.

That night, as I returned to my attic completely alone, I passed, as always, by the Quiñoneses' house. In spite of myself, I felt compelled to stop on the corner and gaze at it for a long time. It was an unremarkable house. An iron gate opened onto an unkempt, weed-ridden garden with a few arum lilies and roses of Castile sticking out here and there from the uncut grass. The front door was a simple wooden rectangle. And inside, as in any other house, there was a living room, a dining room, a kitchen, three bedrooms, and two bathrooms. I saw it from the outside and imagined it on the inside, and no matter how you looked at it, it was the same house. Suddenly, however, I found myself weeping. I felt an urge to go in as before, and I was just about to do so, but I stopped short at the last moment. Then I ran out of the garden and up the street, and, in the blink of an eye, I came running back down the street again.

"Teresa!" I shouted from the sidewalk, but there was no answer. "Genoveva!" I cried as I tried to jump over the gate, but my voice disappeared into a vacuum of utter silence. When I understood that it was all pointless, that everything was lost, I started crying like a baby on their doorstep. At some point, I don't know when, I fell asleep.

At dawn, my whole body ached. Like a convalescent, I got up slowly, stood there, immobile and unblinking, and observed the house, under the influence of what Teresa used to refer to as melancholy.

It's true: I was tormented by the entire presence of the house, but what tormented me most was the possibility of its absence. Nobody would believe me. That was the only thing I could think of for a long time: No one is going to believe me. No man is going to believe me. No woman. I was already beginning to doubt it myself. That's why I ran away once more, under the harsh light of the morning sun. I bounded up the staircase to my attic, and, almost out of breath, I grabbed a pencil and a sheet of paper and wrote down all the words that I knew from Teresa. Thus, I began this account on the 13th of August, 1995, at 6:35 A.M. As soon as I finished it, I ran out again and headed for the soccer fields. Patricio's friends gave me a noisy welcome, and before long

I joined their ranks. We played well and won that day. When the last whistle signaled the end of the game, we ran toward one another. We hugged each other amid smiles and curses, and, later, we sat down to have a few beers. We smelled of sweat.

Little by little, as they told jokes and went on with the celebration, I stopped listening to them. The wail of a siren disappeared in the distance. I thought to myself that Genoveva must be arriving home at that moment. Then, I leaned back on the grass and, looking up, I noticed that autumn was just beginning because there was a strange golden luster on the eucalyptus leaves.

We sit late, watching the dark slowly unfold:
No clock counts this.
TED HUGHES, "SEPTEMBER"

TRANSLATED BY ALEX ROSS

PART III

LA FRONTERA MÁS DISTANTE
(2008)

Autoethnography with the Other

1. Scene of arrival

The man never revealed his name. Perhaps he didn't know it or perhaps he had decided to hide it. Maybe it had never occurred to him that someone else would want to find it. To know.

He appeared one winter morning, lying on the frozen lawn in the backyard. A slight aroma of alcohol on his lips.

[The aroma was, from the start, merely imaginary.]

I observed him for a long time, astonished. I'd stopped in front of the window for no reason, distractedly, with a cup of hot tea in my hands. I would do this often. I was thinking about winter. I was cold. I avoided answering the phone. It was a Sunday.

Undoubtedly, that's why I imagined the smell of alcohol. Surely, because of that I noticed the pale pink color of his lips. Certainly, that's why I stayed still. A statue. Winter Sundays lend themselves to this.

When he opened his eyes, his eyes opened me.

The words that surrounded this apparition were: Gray. Enclosed by eyelashes. Full of wind. Big.

His eyes were all that.

I wanted to run away. I tried to turn my back on him. I tried to return.

[Statue.]

The man raised a hand, and, with the tips of his fingers touching the fingernails of his other hand, he pointed to his open mouth. Then with the forefinger of his right hand he pointed to his stomach. I didn't know what to do, how to react. It must have been my lack of response that caused him to join his palms together and place them, as if beseeching or in prayer, just under his chin. His very center.

The man knew about need, and about supplication, of that I had no doubt.

II. A very brief history of classic ethnography

1. European and North American ethnography—beginning of the twentieth century to the First World War. Characteristics: the solitary ethnographer. Objectivity. Complicity with colonialism. Field work in the periphery: Africa, Asia, the Americas.

2. Modernist anthropology: post-war to the 1970s. Search for the "laws" and "structures" of social life. Social realism.

3. The anthropology of political awareness: 1970–1980. Interpretation of cultures. Radical critiques: feminist, political, reflexive. Mea culpa: anthropologists question their complicity with colonial processes.

III. Language

"I," I'd tell him, pointing to my chest.
    "I," he'd repeat, pointing to my chest.
    "No, I am your you," I'd respond. Gripped by wonder. Peeved.
    "You," he would conclude, pointing to his chest.

IV. Something indescribable, something transparent

During the first three weeks the man moved very slowly through the house. Cautiously, as if he had just recovered from a long illness and was not used to his own body, as if he were an adolescent; or, as if he really came, as I sensed or imagined, from The Outskirts, he exhibited an unusual staggering that made him totter on the floor instead of walk. If seen from afar, it would have been easy to think he was drunk. He would also spend a lot of time motionless, looking at the ceiling. Whenever he started to move, following me with his tottering from room to room, the man would look insistently and somewhat apprehensively behind doors, under the armchairs in the living room, inside corners (when he looked at them, corners did indeed have an inside). He seemed to sense the presence of someone else. He seemed to be distrustful. Perhaps that was why he didn't speak.

His silence, at times interrupted by sudden incomprehensible enunciations, pleased me. I didn't want to know, because I was aware that, knowing, I would end up opening the door for him and that he would disappear in the same way he had arrived: at night, anonymously, without warning. Also, his presence, which I associated with the cold and famine that winter unleashed in The Outskirts, not only suited me, it was interesting. Though dangerous, the man's presence in my house drew in, for the first time, the unknown. In the city, where everyone knew everything, where nothing could be ignored, there was nothing like an enigma to sharpen awareness, your vision, all your senses. Nothing like an enigma to feel alive and alert. For that reason, I was always observing him. Soon, days and hours, at least the ones that I spent at home, became for me pure observation. Sometimes from the corner of my eye, or other times shamelessly, sometimes methodically, or by pure chance, I'd watch him doing and undoing, moving, staying still. I suppose I called him the Stranger because even though he did recognizable things, his actions seemed alien. Because the man was my Lack-of-Comprehension. In reality, he was my Lack.

He preferred the dark—that was clear from the beginning. And he also preferred lean foods. He hated salt. It was enough for me to note the thinness of his body, and the rapid, perhaps desperate way he would place food in his mouth, to know that eating had not been a frequent occurrence in his life; it was an activity that, in any case, afforded him scant pleasure. His squalid figure added to the impression that he was constantly on guard. Whenever he saw a shadow near the windows, even when he'd drawn the curtains himself, a glint of alarm would appear in his eyes. He'd withdraw then to some other place. The attitude of an animal that flees. That's what he seemed like: an animal taking off. An animal that tries to escape its impending punishment. The suffering. He had the same reaction to any sounds or movements that he wasn't completely familiar with. At times it was easy to imagine that violence stalked him.

From the start, the Stranger showed great interest in household devices. He understood perfectly when I warned him that because the water was contaminated, he shouldn't drink it from the tap, but he was capable of spending an entire morning investigating how a fruit juicer functions, or the secret mechanism that caused the iron to expel steam. He'd listen to music with his arms on his chest and his eyes closed: a withdrawal into oneself that recalled a religious experience. Soon, however, the television replaced all that. It became his passion. The TV images, to be more precise, since as soon as I walked away, the Stranger would hurriedly lower the volume. He could laugh, groan, shout, moan for hours on end in front of mute people who raised their arms or moved their lips. On one occasion, upon raising the volume with the remote control, the man covered his ears with both hands and with very quick jumps retreated to a corner of the sofa. The trembling of his body made him whimper uncontrollably. Curled up on the sofa with tears in his eyes, he made that begging motion again. Something indescribable. Something transparent.

v. Postmodern ethnography

1. Crisis of representation 1986–1990: reflexive/narrative movement. Theories on race, class, gender. The centrality of the concept of "culture" is displaced. What "field work" consists of is questioned. Poetry and politics are inseparable.

2. Current postmodernity: universal theories replace local theories. To write ethnography is a conscious and participatory process. Ethnographies are read and commented on by "study subjects." The permission of participants is essential.

3. Ethnographic authority and authenticity: identity between and among subjects. Autoethnography.

vi. The wind from his impassive eyes messes up my hair

"Where are you from?" I'd ask him from time to time, seemingly distracted but with an unfamiliar edge in my own voice. "What's your name?" I insisted in murmurs, gritting my teeth.

"Tell me something," I'd ask him afterwards, beseeching, just as he did, I thought. That look. At that moment the wind from his impassive eyes would mess up my hair.

This: The image of a palm tree almost completely bent by the hurricane's violent wind. A gray day. A tremendously gray day. A winter day.

VII. Cinema, colonialism, and anthropology were born at the same time (1)

Robert Flaherty, *Nanook of the North*, 1922.

Black and white. The open tundra. The wind over it; through it. The silence of the ice. In 1920 the anthropologist Robert Flaherty traveled to the Canadian tundra to study the culture of the Eskimos, and when he recorded this experience in images, Flaherty fostered the birth of documentary cinema. Since then, we've learned that although *Nanook of the North* was presented as directed, produced, and filmed by Flaherty, those responsible for many of the documentary's images were the Eskimos themselves. Nanook, moreover, was posing.

Taxidermic ethnography expresses the desire of some scholars to make what is dead seem alive. Cinema, colonialism, and anthropology were born at the same time.

viii. Bilingual quote (Author's translation)

Escribir etnografía le ofrece *al autor* la oportunidad de reencontrase con el Otro de manera "segura," así como de hallar significado en el caos de la experiencia vivida a través de la reordenación del pasado. Es una especie de odisea proustiana en la cual el etnógrafo trata de encontrar significado en eventos cuya importancia era más bien elusiva en el momento en que se estaban viviendo.

Dorinne Kindo, "Disolución y reconstitución del Yo. Implicaciones para una epistemología antropológica."

Writing ethnography offers *the author* the opportunity to reencounter the Other "safely," to find meaning in the chaos of lived experience through retrospectively ordering the past. It is a kind of Proustian quest in which the ethnographer seeks meaning in events whose significance was elusive while they were being lived.

Dorinne Kindo, "Dissolution and Reconstitution of Self: Implications for Anthropological Epistemology."

ix. On the eleventh day the man cut his nails

He had taken a bath on the fifth day of his stay, but he'd refused to use the nail clipper, running away as soon as I brandished it in front of his face. He only agreed to use the instrument when, after going through all the rooms of the house for the thousandth time, he became convinced that there wasn't, and wouldn't be, anybody else in the surrounding area. It took him a whole afternoon to cut his fingernails. Another to cut his toenails. When he had finished, he ran to me happily and, with the docile movements of a domesticated animal, placed his hand on my hair.

x. On the twenty-fourth day, the man smiled

What happened before had been a chance movement of his face, a disarrangement of his lips, a twitch. But on the twenty-fourth day, as I was putting lipstick on his mouth, and mascara on his eyelashes, the man smiled. It was a Wednesday afternoon. An unusually cold day. All of this in front of a mirror.

xi. On the thirty-eighth day the man discovered money

The first time he touched a coin, he did it gently. Next to his skin that had turned almost white, nearly transparent, due to lack of sunlight, the coin shone as if it were gold. Pure gold. It was very heavy. It gave the impression of being worth a lot.

And he placed the coin on his lips, on his chest. On his genitals. Then he laughed again. And again.

xii. On the thirty-eighth day the man touched another body

I had forgotten what pleasure was. That kind of pleasure. What happens when the fingers of an other's hands—I don't know what these fingers are feeling—rest, with their own temperature, their own exile, their own nerve endings, on your skin. Inside.

Barbara Myerhoff, *Number Our Days*, 1978; *In Her Own Time*, 1986: Anthropology of what surrounds us, within the very context of anthropology. I had forgotten all this:

The weight of another body on one's body—the immobility that this triggers, the beginning of suffocation, claustrophobia. The impulse to run.

> 1. The unequivocality of penetration—the way the erect penis, suddenly solid, in all appearances indestructible, opens what has to be opened. The impulse to run.
> 2. Breathing. Impulse.
> 3. The most personal reverberations of sound. Beyond words.
> 4. Interior sound. (Im)pulse.
> 5. Taste. Pulse.
> 6. Pulse. Agitation.

Marlon Riggs, *Tongues Untied*, 1989. Anthropology and film of one's own body.

XIII. Language again.

"You," he announced in the middle of winter.

"You," he said, pointing to his breastbone. Then he placed himself behind me and started tearing off my clothes. His moans on the back of my neck. His teeth on my shoulders. His saliva on my vertebrae. His pleasure.

"You," he whispered. "You."
Breathing.
It was still the thirty-eighth day.

xiv. Cinema, colonialism, and anthropology were born at the same time (ii)

Margaret Mead, *Bathing Babies in Three Cultures*, 1952.

Black and white. Produced, directed, and narrated by Margaret Mead, this early example of ethnographic cinema shows everything that the anthropologist saw, and all her interpretations regarding the ways three women from different places and cultures—a village in Bali, Iatmul de Sepik in New Guinea, and the United States in 1950—bathe their babies. A comparative vision.

Taxidermic ethnography expresses the desire of some scholars to make what is dead seem alive. Cinema, colonialism and anthropology were born at the same time.

xv. Anthropology and context

"Don't tell me you've got a guy in your house," she said as she peeled an orange, examining rather than looking at me with her dark round eyes full of sorrow, or of nothing. Surely there was a hint of alarm in her voice, but there was also curiosity, mischievousness, perversion. The desire to know and the desire to peek through.

I could have said, "And so what if I had a guy in my house?"

I could have said, "What do you care."
I could have said, "And wouldn't you like to have one?"
I could have burst out laughing.

But I said:

"Of course not!" in that quick, immediate way our culture uses to cover up the guilt we feel when we lie but that never completely succeeds, rather it achieves just the opposite. That is: reproducing the guilt and the lie, and the immediacy of the two combined. At any rate, I said it so convincingly that I almost came to believe it while she continued to peel the orange very slowly, in an almost ritualistic way, producing a very long piece of peel approximately a centimeter wide, which, as the orange wedges were exposed, fell on the floor, as solid things do, succumbing to gravity. One sole strip. A strip of peel that filled the room with a pungent, light, almost adolescent aroma. Oranges. Ah, oranges in winter, its only compensation.

"The girls have started to say things," she paused, and, searching for my eyes as I gazed at the fruit, she continued, "you know."

"What things?" I asked without really wanting to, and because of that, because it had been an automatic reaction, she looked at me as if she were right in front of Nanook or the Balinese mother bathing her baby. I mean, she looked at me with that type of condescension, with that kind of mistrustful distance.

"What do you mean 'what things'?" she exclaimed, exasperated. Then, just as suddenly, she calmed down. "It would be terrible, you know that, don't you? Simply awful."

Then she opened the orange and, with a skillful movement of her hands, pulled out the first wedge. A drop of juice, a drop of something that seemed from a distance to be very sweet, ran down the back of her hand. On her skin.

"Yes," I managed to whisper. "I know."

Somewhere a palm tree. The wind against it. All around. The wind.

When she finished peeling the orange, she offered me one of the wedges, and then, unperturbed by my refusal, as if she hadn't even noticed, she placed it in her mouth full of bright white teeth. The process of grinding.

xvi. James Clifford, et al., *Writing Culture*, 1986

The essays suggest that anthropology is a form of writing, of narrating, of creating literature about the representation of the other.

Field work and the text that emerges from this encounter is a negotiation through which one arrives at an accord about "textual power" and how it will be shared between the anthropologist and the subject.

They assert that feminist anthropology has not contributed anything to experimental and literary ethnography.

Mary Louise Pratt's argument: all ethnography forms part of a rhetorical system. In ethnographies, for example, there exists the convention of "the contact zone"—the key moment of the anthropologist's arrival at the exotic place.

xvii. Illiteracy

He would come to my desk and, looking over my shoulder, he'd try to see what I was writing on the black lines of the page in my notebook. My behavior at such moments was unusual: instead of closing it, I'd smile at him and bring it closer to his face. As I did that—opening the notebook, showing it to him—I wondered if I would have done it, if I'd have dared to do it, if he had known how to read. I wondered if his intrusion would have provoked such pleasure, such laughter. In this way, I realized that I trusted in his ignorance as much as in mine. His ignorance prevented me from feeling afraid or offering resistance. His ignorance was half of our salvation. The other half was my own ignorance.

xviii. Watching

The Woman With the Orange knocked on my door on a Wednesday afternoon. I had just gotten home from the institute where I was doing my anthropological research, and because of that my eyes were tired, and I was in a rotten mood. I had already drunk a glass of water and taken off my coat and shoes. I had massaged my neck. When I heard the knocking on the door, I wanted to run to warn him. And that's what I did. I went through the entire house until I found him. He looked at me with that wind that blew my hair before hurrying, bent over, toward my bedroom closet. Like an animal that flees. Like an animal awaiting punishment.

"You probably think my visit odd," the woman affirmed as soon as I opened the door.

"That's true," I quickly replied, without inviting her in, visibly alarmed. "Is something wrong? Did something happen?"

I thought she would answer me. I thought she'd make up some excuse to justify her presence. I thought, at the very least, she'd ask permission to enter my space. But the woman came in and looked around the living room with a freedom I had not granted her.

"Since we've hardly seen you recently, I thought it would be a good idea to pay you a visit," she murmured while she took off her gloves and undid her scarf. "I thought perhaps you needed to talk with someone you trust."

Her coming left me motionless by the side of the half-open door with my hand around the doorknob. From there I observed her comings and goings in the living room, the scandalous way she sniffed around corners, angles, windows.

"I'm tired," I said, because I didn't know what else to say. And also because it was true.

The woman sat next to me and put her hand on my knee.

xix. Cinema, colonialism, and anthropology were born at the same time (iii)

Ishi, the Last Yahi, 1967.

In August of 1911, Ishi, the last surviving Yahi, left the hills near Mount Lassen, the area where his tribe had hidden for approximately forty years. From 1911 to 1916, the year in which he died of tuberculosis, Ishi lived in the Anthropology Museum of the University of California, San Francisco, sharing information about his culture and his language with the anthropologists

Alfred Kroeber and Theodore T. Waterman and the surgeon Saxton T. Pope. During those years, Ishi participated in recording Yahi myths, songs, and cultural narratives, which form part of this black-and-white ethnographic film.

Taxidermic ethnography expresses the desire of some scholars to make what is dead seem alive. Cinema, colonialism, and anthropology were born at the same time.

xx. The end of the private world

It was a Sunday when I took him with me to the movies. I wanted to have fun, it's true, but I also wanted to see his reaction. His relationship to images, his reaction to sound, his position as spectator intrigued me. Besides, I also needed some air. I wanted to see him in other contexts. I wanted to make him real. The movie theatre offered the protection of darkness, the almost certain possibility of anonymity. If the Stranger and I were to go unnoticed it could only be at the movies. That great theatre of the world.

I applied make-up on him as I had done a few times before, in private, in front of the bathroom mirror. I can't remember how many times we had almost died laughing while playing the language game; how many times our pointing "I" and "You" erroneously had made us angry at each other. How often we had kept quiet, impassive in the face of our own reflexes, our own probabilities? When, at the end of the ritual, I put gloss on his lips, I felt an almost biological sadness: all that coming to an end. I knew it. I knew it and my body knew it. Our entire private world was coming to an end. And even then, I kept on. Now, outside, the two of us would certainly become known to others, but above all we would become known to ourselves. The melancholy and the mourning that I began to feel for our vanished privacy, however, did not deter my curiosity. I wanted to see him outside of me. I wanted to experience that distance.

And that's how it was. I saw him. He walked by my side but not near me. He walked by my side but within himself, bound to his vision of the city, to his own wonder. Unleashed, in reality. He gazed greedily, as if he were touching everything with his eyes. As if everything that was touched produced pleasure. He collided into other pedestrians, he'd look at them and, just like a savage, just like a cannibal, he'd consume them in that very moment of sudden contemplation. A wedge of orange in a mouth. A drop of sweet liquid on skin. He walked rapidly and took in big gulps of air. He smiled often. He was overcome with emotion. Emotion was destroying him. In the cinema it was hard for him to keep quiet, to stay still. But when the theatre went dark and the first image appeared, he became completely motionless. An almost religious paralysis kept him glued to his chair until the credits finished rolling.

"Me," he whispered at the end, with an impassive expression, pointing to his chest.

"You," I managed to stammer before the lights came on.

He had the look of a sad woman. That grimace.

XXI. What do you call a letter you never sent?

I read *Translated Woman: Crossing the Border with Esperanza's Story* many years ago in a state of pure fervor. I was preparing then for my doctoral exams in anthropology and, for that reason, more out of obligation than for pleasure, I was going over at least three books each week on my topic: borders, otherness, violence. The multiple ways in which we write them. In which we go through them, surrendering and withholding at the same time. In which we honor them. In which we suffer them. I of course read everything published on the topic, but I was also reviewing publications in other scientific disciplines as well as anything else that combined them, or that came across my path. That's how Esperanza, a peddler in a nondescript town in central Mexico, and with her, Ruth Behar, the autoethnographer, came into my house. It was about nine at night when I opened the book. How many decades between the moment it was written and the moment it crossed the threshold of my eyes? Too many. An eternity, perhaps. At about three in the morning in a state of perplexity, I began to write a letter, a stammering, celebratory, very long letter to an author who a century before had seen it worth her while to converse with another woman and note down in great detail the information and the gaps in information from their talks. Of course, I never sent the letter, but I remember having seen that dawn with other eyes.

XXII. Hungry, vengeful, effective

I knew, of course, that it was a possibility. The city wasn't very big, and on weekends during winter, going to the movies was almost natural, even mandatory. We could have gone to the lake, I suppose. Or waited until the midnight showing. Or not gone anywhere, just stayed together, inside the house, day after day, night after night, forever. I had heard that some very stubborn or determined women had managed on occasion, and in places not very far from the city where I lived, to do something like that: live shut up with another person for many years, for a whole lifetime even. I also suppose that if I didn't do that, it was because I wanted to be found out. I didn't have a choice. Undoubtedly, I wanted to be seen. When shortly after returning home I got a call from the Woman With the Orange, I wasn't surprised. Nor was I afraid.

"We saw you today," she said. Then, because I didn't reply, she added, "You've been lying to us."

At that moment I was looking at the Stranger who was lying down in front of the window, just as immobile as he had been in front of the screen, observing the world. Outside the world was covered with a thin layer of ice.

"Yes," I assented in a very low voice.

"But how could you . . ." stammered the other woman. Then, in response to my silence, she hung up.

I went over and hugged him. We stayed like that for a long time, embracing each other. And that's how they found us when they kicked in the apartment door.

Their fuss didn't separate us. On the contrary. Their arrival forced us to hug each other more firmly, with more fear. I curled up within his chest. At times, he did the same.

Finally, one of the women said:

"You should have told us about this finding. Did you know that?"

I nodded without showing my face. The man smelled of fear, of lip gloss, of false eyelashes.

"Punishment. Do you know what the punishment is for what you've done?"

I nodded again, this time looking at them.

"Yes, I know," I repeated. I thought of the palm tree that in some other part of the world was bending under a powerful hurricane gale. A gray day. A cold day. Then I saw his eyes and the wind—that wind—messed up my hair.

"And even then . . ." her astonishment was so great that she was unable to finish the sentence.

"Even then," I said, trying to take my hair out of my eyes, lying. In reality, I didn't know. I had heard—because it was inevitable—all the rumors about what might happen, but I had always refused to fully know. When, as was their custom, the foremothers told those macabre stories, I shut my ears thinking it was better not to know. I thought that if I knew I could never manage to have enough courage, or to be bold enough. I thought that, if I didn't know, when the time came I would dare. From that moment I was on the side of unknowing, and I defended it by calling it the enigma. But now unknowing was lashing out at me. And the truth, the truth that I had refused to accept from the beginning, was laughing at me. It was seeking revenge.

The rest happened too fast. One of the women began to take photographs of the Stranger, of both of us together, clutching one another, while the others searched for proof of his living in my house. Clothes. Videos. Notes. Messages. Anything. They were the authorities but acted as criminals. In fact, they behaved as a horde of savages. Hungry, vengeful, effective. The women moved with great precision around the tight space of the apartment, and with their hurried work they made it seem even smaller. Soon nothing was left intact. Soon, they'd catalogued everything. The first thing that they put away in a big plastic bag was my notebook with the black lines.

"Where will you take him?" I asked when the Stranger, with that look that was both indescribable and transparent, was led to the door in handcuffs.

"Where we always take them," said the Woman With the Orange, winking at me. I was going to ask what place that was, but at the last moment I realized that to ask this question would incriminate me, revealing that I'd intentionally shut my ears to the truth. Our truth. It would be even worse than admitting I had opened the doors of my home to the Stranger. I realized that despite the expression I knew so well in him, the look that had indeed been the key with which he'd entered my house, I would let him go. I realized that if I had known things would be like this, that they were always like this, I would never have been bold or dumb enough to open the door.

"Does it have to be this way?" I said, trying a last appeal. Begging, really.

"You know it does."

When the raid was over, I made a cup of tea and, holding it with both hands, went to the window. I stood there for a long time. If no trace had remained of his body's silhouette on the icy grass I would have convinced myself that the Stranger had been imaginary. But there it was, next to the bare walnut tree, to the side of the curving gravel path that brought visitors to my door. There it was: a slight imperfection in the grass's consistency. Something that only a good observer would detect.

XXIII. Punishment

I didn't find out that he knew how to read until much later, when normality reestablished itself in my house. When once again I took long, silent walks. When I returned to the backyard to prepare the soil for summer vegetables. It was then, while cleaning the sofa on which he'd once curled up, paralyzed by the sheer terror that sound produced, that I discovered the sheet of paper. Without a doubt it was from my notebook with the black lines.

It said: "Punishment is this: this."

It was the writing of someone who had recently become literate, or of someone in constant flight. A resident from the Outskirts. One of them.

Everything went back to normal afterward. I read. I boiled my grains. I participated in the community garden. I once again worked with discipline, with pleasure even. Every now and then, I got together with the women who shared you-know-what-kind-of-secrets in dimly lit places as we trimmed the tops and bottoms of the oranges, cut off the peels with a sharp knife, removed as much of the white pith as possible, and cut alongside each one of the white lines so that the segments came right out. We gulped them, voraciously, paying little attention to manners. Laughter overtook us quite often, a maddening sound that haunted us for days to come. Our sticky fingers. The cigarettes we smoked when all was done. I awaited summer just as they did: the few days of summer. I began to use the same teacup. Once in a while, I would read the letter that the man had written unbeknownst to me, in one of the few moments I didn't see him. It said only one thing. It said: "Punishment is this: this."

Tautological.

XXIV. Retro-translation

Beacon Press reedited *Translated Woman* years later, something that was rather unusual with "academic" texts, and the book, as one of its authors said, not only found its way beyond university campuses and into places as unexpected as the cells of certain nameless prisons, it was also adapted for the stage. Later, the book made the return trip from English, into which portions had been translated back to Spanish, the "original" language. Undoubtedly it was a retro-translation—the return to an origin that was, from the beginning, the false origin. The return as a trajectory of what, finally, is gone, masking itself. A meaning with wings.

xxv. Museum of Anthropology of the University of California, San Francisco, 1911–1916

Sometimes Ishi looks through the window. This way.
[Black-and-white ethnographic film.]

Taxidermic ethnography expresses the desire of some scholars to make what is dead seem alive. Cinema, colonialism, and anthropology were born at the same time.

TRANSLATED BY FRANCISCA GONZÁLEZ ARIAS

Carpathian Mountain Woman

*Write this. We have burned all their villages. Write this. We have
burned all their villages and the people in them. Write this. We have
adopted their customs and their manner of dress.*
MICHAEL PALMER, "SUN," CODES APPEARING

"I first came here twenty years ago," I answered softly as I pretended not to notice his intense blue gaze. He didn't believe me. That's what I assumed—that he didn't believe me; so I went on to tell him I'd arrived on the back of a gray donkey with a bit of food and a couple of notebooks. He put a blade of grass between his teeth and said nothing. The hint of a smile between his lips. The sky as blue as his eyes. The wind.

"And you've been dressing like a man ever since?"

I remembered how he had taken me: violently. A stray longing in each hand. A private fury. His fingers like can openers in my mouth. How long I had gone without seeing an artifact like that! I remembered the smell of his sweat, vaguely carnivorous. And the bitter taste of his cheeks. Still bent over the river and still pretending not to see his intense blue gaze, I told him it was better to live alone as a man. He didn't ask me why I said that. He picked up his small leather satchel and started to leave. I counted his steps without turning to look at him. When he got to number twenty-three, he hesitated. He turned around.

"Will you wait for me?" he asked.

"Yes," I said, still bent over the river water. I put my hand in the current and pulled out a smooth, round stone. I held it in front of me as if it were a mirror. Then I slipped it into the right-hand pocket of my trousers. I thought I would want to remember that afternoon. I thought the stone was in place of the stranger.

I never knew why I had mentioned that number: twenty years. I also didn't know what it was he'd made me promise to wait for.

Before choosing my destiny, I had read about them. A strange book, half history, half legend. A book from a library in the city. I read it immoderately, as I used to do in those days. With the moistened tip of my index finger perpetually poised to turn the page, I forgot to eat. I only stopped occasionally to take a sip of water, but I never actually drank it; as soon as I put the rim of the glass to my lips, I would become distracted again. Something urgent called to me from across the room, and I answered the call. Before closing the book, I had already made up my mind: I would leave that place—that kitchen, that library, that city. I would become someone else. One of them. It's difficult to explain why one does the things one does. But everything happened just like it does in books: I left that place, and, almost without a plan, I showed up in a small village where they needed men. I put on my new clothes and committed myself to a life of celibacy. And they, who were so few, bowed their heads when I passed.

The stranger showed up in front of my door one day at around noon. He didn't arrive, as I once had, on the back of a donkey, but on the battered seat of a military vehicle. A mud-spattered windshield. Four thick tires. A torn canvas roof. The letters on the door made no sense to me, but the words he spoke to me did. He asked me for water, and, since I didn't move, he opened his canteen and turned it upside down.

"Do you understand me?" he repeated, with growing exasperation. "I need water."

I hadn't seen anyone like him for a long time. His gestures, so childlike, so unnecessary, moved me. He seemed to be afraid of dying.

"Where are you from?" I asked him, trying to make him feel less uncomfortable as he stood there in the doorway. Perhaps I was already trying to dissuade him, to distract him. I've never known how to get rid of people. When he gave a start, which he attempted to conceal, I realized that he couldn't see me well. My house, like all mountain houses, was small and dark. Later, he would refer to it as "the shack." Cool in the summer, warm in the winter. That's why our houses are that way.

"So you're a woman," he whispered in a tone expressing both surprise and amusement. His body was blocking the sun, so I couldn't see him well either. I didn't know how to answer. Then he crossed the threshold. A long and voluminous stride. I was very slow to react.

He talked about the war. When he finished gulping down the water, he wiped his mouth with his sleeve and sat down at the table. He asked for food. He asked for more.

"What's that?" he asked when he heard the sound of the bells.

"A mass," I said as I set a plate with pieces of meat in front of him. "Part of a funeral," I murmured later.

He ate the same way he had drunk a few minutes earlier: eagerly. Voraciously. He ate the food with his hands and he lifted it to his mouth without turning to look at anything else. Then he chewed and swallowed noisily. Then he sucked his fingers clean.

When he'd had his fill, he began to talk. He lit a pipe and talked, without stopping, about the war. The words flowed from his mouth just as the food had entered it a few moments earlier: in a deluge. He told about the years of his life. He saw the adolescent he had been, thoughtful and serene. He heard gunshots, the echo of gunshots. He felt thirst. A relentless sun once more wrinkled his skin, blinded his eyes, dried his lips. He swallowed dirt. He desperately craved the taste of salt on his tongue. He was hypnotized by the color of fire. He walked for entire nights, climbing hills and descending them again, soaked with urine and with fear. He shot. He closed his eyes and shot. Many times.

"You don't know what it's like," he said. And then, without waiting for a reply, he continued. The cold. The filth. The smell of rotting flesh. Death. He relived it all again. A small body beneath the infinite, maddening sky.

"You're never more vulnerable than when you're under the sky," he insisted.

I offered him some liquor because he seemed to need it. The noise of the bottle touching the wood broke his concentration. He looked at me again. He must have been wondering who I was, what I was doing here, where we actually were, but he didn't ask any questions. He drank the liquor in small sips. After a while, he fell asleep with his head on the table.

Every forest always has another forest inside of it. The one on the inside is the mythical, enchanted forest found in fairy tales. Living in the outside forest, however, is not easy. Life in the mountains requires effort, discipline, sacrifice. Above all, you need to have good hands. And it never hurts to have a level head on your shoulders, one that's accustomed to solitude. You need to cut down trees, plant seeds, use frigid water from the rivers. There can be fires. There are bears, and eagles, and other frightening animals. Sometimes, toward the end of winter, everything is covered with snow. And you have to walk on the snow, keep moving forward. Sometimes it's good to be able to recognize the sound of a breaking branch. It's good to walk, slowly, on the dry leaves. Sometimes you take a deep breath. Sometimes everything stops. But more than anything else, there's work in the forest, lots of work. Fairytales rarely mention that.

"And you can do all that by yourself?" he asked me later.

I told him the truth: I told him No. That I couldn't do all that by myself. And my answer seemed to satisfy him.

"Do the local men come to help you?"

"As often as I help them," I told him, defiantly. Or it seemed to me that my tone of voice was defiant.

He returned to that topic many times, each time from a different angle, as if he couldn't find the best way to ask what he wanted to ask.

"Every forest always has another forest inside of it," I murmured when he got out of bed and went to the window and stood there with an attitude of expectation. He stayed that way, very still, for a long time. When he turned around to look at me, I lowered my eyes. Then I covered my shoulders with the blanket. Then I said:

"You shouldn't be here."

Why does someone grab a pair of notebooks, take a long trip on a dilapidated hulk of a bus, get off in a distant province, and then travel on the back of a donkey for days and days in order to reach, if they possibly can, the remotest spot imaginable? I don't know. Why does someone choose a forest? I can't answer that either. There is the green, of course. The abundance of greens that are the color green. You have to learn how to see. There's the fresh air and the sky, this sky-blue sky. The solitude of the sky. No one is ever more defenseless than when they know they are alone under the sky. The possibility of remaining silent for hours at a time, days at a time, months at a time. The possibility of forgetting how to write. The possibility of not speaking. There are the extended, callused, dry, brutal hands that can take up tools to cut, plant, plow. There is the voice: deep. The echo, also deep. The possibility of saying, "We have burned all the villages. We have burned all the villages and the people in them. We have adopted their customs and their way of dress." The laughter inside the church walls during the rites. The slow walking down the aisle, the shaking of hands, the endless bowing of heads. There is the crying of babies being born: a deep echo. Another. There is the beginning: the oldest forest. The forest inside the forest. That promise. Listen to this: there is the inescapable fact that we have burned all the villages and the people in them.

You can't live in the forest without having a theory of the forest. During burials, when I join the funeral procession, and later, when I look inside the coffin at the dead person's face, it's impossible to avoid wondering if it's worth it. If all of this is worth it. The problem, as always, is the children and the old people. The problem is always the most vulnerable ones. The ones who one fine day abandon the yoke and run as fast as they can among the trees, looking for a little light. Sometimes it gets so dark under the trees. And so cold. The problem is the ones who lose their minds. You stand there looking at the dark pathways and you wonder about the taste of liquor in the mouth of the man who shovels dirt over all that. The forest means: somewhere beyond, everything is in flames. There is a moth that flutters in the air. The blade of the tool has severed the leg. The snow is falling. The nature of snow is to fall. There was snow before; there will be snow afterward. The forest will survive all of that. All of this. In front of the falling house, the illuminated face. An idol. The nature of houses is to fall. The noise of the axe. Soon we will disappear. There is an urgent need to go to the tree. The amputated leg. The trail of blood on the snow. A pair of footprints.

I told him I hadn't been in a city for many years. The last one I saw was the one I'd left behind. Remembering its lights made me blink rapidly. Then I laughed.

"I never went back," I said, stating the obvious. Then I spat out of the left side of my mouth and took another swing at the firewood with my axe. A heavy thud. The smell of sweat. A flying bird. The stranger stepped back. It was the first time he did that.

"Show me your hands," he ordered instead of asking. "Do you see that?" he asked derisively, pointing at my splinters and my broken nails. "You could never live in the city looking like that."

His presumption annoyed me, especially since it was false. It bothered me that he thought I might want to return. That I would be interested in going back to all that. A woman with red hands. A Carpathian mountain woman. So I turned away from him and continued chopping the firewood into smaller and smaller pieces. I could hear my own breathing. My inhaling and exhaling. I concentrated on the movement of my wrists. I had to be taut and perfect, without vacillating. The shifting of my weight from one leg to the other. The vertical length of my arms. My back. Soon I settled into a familiar rhythm. My body inside its own choreography. My body inside the forest within.

"You shouldn't have come back," I whispered, my voice barely audible against the clamor of my agitated breathing. "Why did you?"

"People migrate; it's natural," he answered, also with his back turned.

While it was happening, while all of this was taking place, I imagined the bodies engulfed in flames. Those visions interrupted my dreams. They interrupted my waking hours as well. They interrupted my theory of the forest.

"They never learned our language," said some, in an attempt at self-justification. And all of this inside the church.

"They looked down on our dances," argued others, as the bells rang softly.

"Did you notice that they never bow their heads?"

The forest is always expanding.

People kept asking the same questions. Offering the same justifications. It didn't matter that others spoke of connecting rivers. Any attempt to explain about context, about the vital importance of context for the dissemination of our language, fell on deaf ears. There is something larger. Would we understand ourselves without others who don't understand us? There is something that contains us. These types of questions always provoked a general irritation. Widespread grumbling.

Within the church, one heard: "We burned their villages." It was a deep echo, a very soft voice. "We burned the people in them. We adopted their customs. Their way of dress."

I looked down and found my hands, orphaned, on my lap.

All around me, the word *wretched*. Touch this.

Civilization is always expanding, and so is barbarism. Between them is the forest: I know. The green. The sky. The snow, which falls. The funeral bells. The blood, the footprint. There is a man in the forest who is a woman. There is a woman. A forest.

I don't know if they did it for me, but I've always wondered about it. It isn't easy to guess other people's intentions. Three more had died: two girls and a boy. There were so few of us. Scarcity leads to strange behavior. The darkness under the trees. Perpetual isolation. Living beyond the pale. Panic is a disease; that's clear. They kept touching the children's foreheads just to make sure the fever would end with them. They tried to decipher their last words. It was a mother who pointed her finger. Panic is a disease, which is a drama. Her crying was a bladed tool that cut me in two. I had lived among them, in fact, for many years. I had served them well. They had the kind of cautious affection for me that one feels toward someone who, because she arrived late, will never penetrate the mystery of the cause. But they didn't view me with suspicion. They bowed their heads when I passed. They sought my opinion. When I broke a leg, they took care of my farm. One summer, they pulled me out of the well I had fallen into. They gave me three lambs, which later became seven, and then fifteen. Eventually, they became wool and also chunks of meat on pewter plates. We ate together. We swallowed in unison. We weren't intimidated by the gleam of each other's teeth or by the weight of our hands on the wooden table. At this table we studied their dress and their customs in my notebooks. It was here that we leafed through the books and saw the pictures. It was here that we planned the fires.

I've spoken their language for as long as I can remember. Don't ask me why someone chooses a forest. I don't have an answer.

Finally, he said, he had remembered. He said he'd seen me, a long time ago, months or maybe even years before my departure. He recognized the notebooks, he said. The black covers. Their unusual size. The hands that held them firmly.

"Do you remember that?" he asked.

Naturally, I answered that I didn't.

That didn't make him stop. He said he had been there, on the opposite sidewalk, standing in the drizzle, while I waited, with the notebooks pressed against my chest, for the bus that would take me far away.

"Now I remember that day perfectly," he assured me.

Of course I shook my head vigorously at this. I must have looked at him with enormous eyes because suddenly he burst out in wild laughter. A bird that flies. I started to laugh without knowing exactly why. This kind of laughter, which soon turns to hilarity, usually leaves me feeling desolate. There's a moment in every story when it's possible to suddenly see what will happen next. I saw it then and there, in the middle of a story invented by a stranger to create a context for a moment that never existed. Inside my desolation. After the laughter.

That's why I kept silent.

Because of this: Outside, the snow would soon be falling again, silently. Little by little, the footsteps would become audible. The rest would happen in a flurry: the struggle, the bladed tool in the air, its irrevocable fall. The body parts. The trickle of blood. The footprints.

He had said, before his wild fit of laughter, that he was like a person who tells a story only to have the privilege, or the power—

this he also said—to introduce a foreign element into it. Something that doesn't quite fit.

I saw him then. I used my hands to expose his face. I saw him absolutely.

"The last day, the day of the drizzle—it didn't exist," I murmured.

It was only then that he kept silent.

It's difficult to explain how one can remain still under the snow for so long. Difficult to say: these are my knees, this is your torso, your thigh; these are your fingers. These are the eyes you looked at me with. People migrate; it's natural. It's always difficult to describe what an axe does. Difficult to witness the outstretched finger of the mother and difficult to hear her howling on the other side of the window and difficult to break in two, very slowly, when one understands the verdict. It's difficult to remain still, with fists clenched, and be a witness to the facts. The branch that rustles. The bird. It is difficult to be under the sky.

When I secretly murmured the word *Carpathian*, I was able to see a forest, a blue sky, and falling snow. I was a little girl then. That's the truth.

TRANSLATED BY ALEX ROSS

City of Men

She arrived in the City of Men one Thursday afternoon, in the middle of winter.

Unlike the passengers who smiled when the airplane landed, she let out a sigh of exhaustion. She closed her eyes, leaned her head against the pillow, and pressed her shoulders into the back of her seat. Before standing up, she glanced once more at the notes she'd written during the flight: a few scribbles outlining a seven-day work plan. Even though she'd asked several times for someone else to be sent in her place, her editor successfully convinced her to pack her bags, find someone to take care of her cat, and carry out the initial investigation. A report on the City of Men from the point of view of a woman would, her editor told her, be a guaranteed success. In any case, she couldn't risk losing her job. She had debts and aspirations, both of which forced her to smile without too much irony when he put the tickets in her hand.

"We will await your return," her boss said as she was walking out the office door, her hand on the doorknob.

"Of course," she said, looking back with apprehension, but his face had already returned to his computer screen.

She showed her official documents at the immigration offices, then reluctantly went for her bags. As she waited, she thought about the sneer on the officer's face. He'd looked her up and down as he asked the reason for her trip. She answered with the truth: work. The officer remained silent, parsimoniously signing the papers without hiding the sneer that crept from his cheek to the left corner of his mouth.

"I'm a journalist," she added, not waiting for him to formulate the question.

"Yes, of course," the officer murmured, his mouth horizontal once again.

Suitcase in hand, she walked toward the last door: the threshold to a place she had never wanted to go. She almost stopped to take it all in before crossing over, but at the last moment she decided to continue as if she had done this many times before. She was distracted, yes, unhappy. She had to force herself forward. The man who strode past her, trying to snatch her bag from her left shoulder, must have noticed. The other man who, running in the opposite direction, tried to take her suitcase, must also have noticed. The wind between the two. The face when it disappears. The smell of deceit. When the third man appeared, repeating her name several times and taking her by the shoulders when she didn't respond, she couldn't do anything but reach out her arm to put some distance between them.

"I'm sorry," she murmured when she realized he was her host.

"These people can be savages," he said, smiling.

The journalist would describe that smile later, in one of her first reports on the city. She would say: "It was more a sneer than a smile, the kind of condescending look the powerful use to prevail upon the weak. At the same time, and this is the subjugating power of that expression, its ambiguity and threat combined, it was a *natural* smile. There was nothing in it that would indicate trickery or calculation, a predetermined plan. The smile spread across his face, candid even, showing a row of bright white teeth."

The Man with the Natural Smile took her suitcase without asking and, overly friendly, guided her toward the airport exit. The journalist sighed. She was finally there: The City of Men. The sky, cloudy. The tall buildings. The wide streets. The rows of cars. The billboards. The lights of the streetlamps. The puddles on the sidewalks. The traffic lights. The drops of water on the windshields. The blurred faces behind all of it.

That night the journalist dreamed she was levitating. She was walking down a narrow street lined with poplars when her feet suddenly lifted from the asphalt. She didn't want to fly. She didn't even know if she could. Her body, however, seemed to be used to gliding, vertically, just above the ground. But this sensation of lightness that at first was exciting soon turned into a feeling of apprehension, and then, almost immediately, of terror. She didn't know when she would stop. She didn't know if she would be able to stop if she wanted to. The deep melancholy of not knowing forced her to open her eyes.

"I should look for her," she told herself quietly, and then, as if she hadn't come out of her dream, she turned over in bed and went back to sleep.

She woke up after nine in the morning. Anemic sunlight filtered through the thin curtains. She stretched her arms. Yawned. Before rising she consulted her agenda for the day: her workday didn't start until the afternoon. She ordered breakfast to her room and turned on the shower. The water gave her an intense feeling of happiness, though she couldn't say why. By the time the food arrived, she was already dressed and made up. She was even flipping through a book by a local poet. She craved coffee.

"And will you be visiting us for long?" the boy asked as he lifted the pot and, with graceful, almost feminine movements, served the first cup. She smiled at him, naïve.

"Not really," she said. "Seven days or so."

He handed her the cup and narrowed his eyes.

"That's what the others said," he whispered. Then he offered her sugar and set about pouring orange juice. Something in her back trembled.

"The others?" she asked without lifting her hands from the pages of the local poet's book.

"The other journalists, of course," he said. "The ones who came before you."

She stared at him. She looked at his shoulders and neck. She ran her eyes over the curves of his butt, his thighs, his shoes. She returned to his hair. He couldn't be older than twenty-one.

"And how long did the others stay?" she couldn't hide the shaking in her voice, the anxiety with which she awaited his response.

"That I don't know," he responded, turning his face toward her, this time offering a brimming glass of orange juice. "But it was longer than they expected."

The journalist drank the juice without taking her eyes off him. Days later, in one of her first reports about that place, she would write: "The man seemed young, but he acted without the spontaneity generally associated with youth. On the contrary, even though he seemed to have come to serve breakfast, his mission was really quite different: it was to let me know it would not be easy to leave the City of Men. What that boy was telling me was that the door in was not necessarily going to be the door out. When I understood the threat, he left. I left him an enormous tip."

"And how many journalists have there been?" I asked before he closed the door.

He smiled again. He gave the impression of having triumphed.

"There were only two," he replied. "Maybe three."

She opened her computer and confirmed the internet wasn't working. She dialed the newspaper a couple of times but on both occasions the connection, once initiated, was cut off. Given she didn't have any interviews until four, she left her room and looked for a way to get to the Central Newspaper Archive. She couldn't think of a better place to look for information on those two or three journalists who had stayed in this place longer than they'd planned. She wondered, as she crossed the streets with hands in her coat pockets, if those women had managed to write their articles. If they'd published them. Indeed, she didn't remember any journalists having been sent to the City of Men, much less any who would have extended their visit enough for a hotel staff member to have noticed it. Her boss, when he'd assured her a report on the city from a woman's point of view would be a great success, hadn't said anything about it. For a moment, as she glimpsed her silhouette in the institution's great glass doors, she laughed at herself. Such was her animosity toward this city that a little boy's comment could fill her with dread.

An old man with a full head of white hair directed her to the room that housed the foreign newspapers. There weren't many— she realized immediately—but she did find the one she worked for. She flipped through some recent issues while the ones from the past were being brought. She'd asked for issues from two years back, from right before she'd been hired for the international section. The man with the white hair brought them just a few minutes later. She scanned the masthead for names she didn't recognize; but she knew them all. She started flipping through, thinking it was all a mistake, feeling embarrassed. So as not to appear ridiculous, she continued reading for a few more minutes. Then, without saying a word, she left the table. She concluded that the boy from the hotel had been playing a trick on her and again crossed the streets that separated her from the hotel. The sky, gray. The glass buildings. The giant billboards. All of that made her walk quickly, looking at the tips of her shoes.

Months later, the unsigned reports that were delivered to the newspaper's office would provide a description of what happened when she opened the door to her room: "The envelope, white and rectangular, contrasted against the dark color of the carpet. It was impossible not to see it. I picked it up: no name. I opened it. The note was short and in tiny, irregular handwriting. *Get out. Leave this place. Soon you will have no way to escape.* I looked out into the hallway, but no one was there. I entered the room and instinctively went to the window. Lots of men were crossing the street and none of them turned their face toward the hotel tower. I sat on the stool, lost in thought. When I looked up, I was frighted by the image I found in the mirror: my face had changed. I was afraid. Minutes later the telephone rang: it was the Man with the Natural Smile, waiting in the lobby to take me to the afternoon interviews: a university professor, a politician, a boxer. I was slow to react. While in the elevator, I realized I had forgotten the recorder, so I went back for it. I noticed the alteration immediately. Everything seemed to be in its place but somehow nothing was. A smell. There was a smell there, in the hotel room, that hadn't been there when I left a few minutes before. The sound of the telephone startled me. 'Is something wrong?' the Man with the Natural Smile asked. I told him I would be downstairs in two seconds."

Nothing she heard in the interviews surprised her. Despite differences in education and class, the University Professor, Representative, and Boxer were all in agreement that their lives in the City of Men were good, healthy, successful. Their relocations from different parts of the world had been, according to the three of them, for the better. Moral crises, all minor, had preceded their respective decisions. The journalist couldn't help but notice the similarity in their stories and the similarities in the smiles that accompanied their otherwise austere, measured gestures. The University Professor gave her his card upon saying goodbye. He invited her to sit in on one of his classes and then, as if he'd just thought of it, let her know he would like to dine with her the next day. His treat. The journalist declined the invitation but took the card. Then, as if she had a lot more to do, she asked her host to take her somewhere with computers that could access the internet.

"There should be some in the hotel," he answered, somewhat puzzled. "They're for the exclusive use of foreigners."

"And the telephone? Yesterday I couldn't contact my offices," she continued, trying not to show her growing concern.

The Smiling Man placed his fingertips on her right elbow and, with great delicacy, led her to the university exit.

"The service can be terrible sometimes," he said by way of an explanation. "In some ways, our city is still a work in progress, as you might imagine," he added. "But you can always use the mail service," he finally said.

That night she was expected at a large dinner party with some artists. She put on something restrained, black, and went down to the dining room. Her host was there, and the ten or twelve artists were already talking animatedly among themselves. In the room people didn't talk about *the city*, but *the project*. The broadness of its streets. The vertical lines of its buildings. The merging of the exciting world of commerce with the search for deeper, more serene spiritual paths. More accessible for all. Its literature. Its poetry. The singular reach of its theater experimentation. The dinner progressed with the kind of conventions the journalist found familiar and tiring. The toast was made by the poet she'd read that morning; she realized that when she recognized his face from the back of the book and, just like the pages that had left her unmoved, his words of praise and welcome felt empty. Otherwise, she enjoyed the food, from the soup that let off an aroma of sage to the duck that tasted of honey. She also enjoyed the glasses of wine that a gloved hand kept filled. They were about to serve dessert when she noticed it: the voices, the scents, the movements. There was something about all of it that, from her position at the head of the table, she found enigmatic and attractive at the same time. The conversations flew at a lighter pace. Without the affected voices from earlier, without the rigidity with which they'd welcomed her and squeezed her hand, they gave the impression of having relaxed and, at the same time, of having gotten younger. All of them, she realized when she took her first sip of the dessert wine, had returned to childhood. Their eyes gave off that definitive gleam of hope or innocence. The volume of their voices had risen. And they were touching one another. Pats on the back. Toasts. The journalist watched for a long time in silence. When she excused herself, she had to accept there was something unresolved in her head.

She had forgotten about it during the dinner, but when she opened the door to her room, it was still there: the smell. Something dense and floral. Something corrupted. Rotten. How could she have thought about anything but that smell for almost three hours? she wondered as she moved very slowly over the carpet, as if worried that, knowing she was trying to locate it, the smell would retreat. She looked under the bed. She went in the bathroom. She opened the dresser drawers. She checked the narrow space of the balcony. She went through her suitcases. She glanced in the closet. She didn't find anything there: there were no leftovers or trash that could cause the stink. There were no dead bugs or dirty clothes. The room was as tidy as it had been when she arrived the day before.

That night the journalist dreamed she was inside an enormous house. In fact, as the dream progressed, the house grew bigger and bigger. She was walking and, instead of getting closer to the back door, which was her objective, the distance she had to walk kept increasing. She calculated there were about three meters left when she walked into a mirror: there was a tiny woman in it. A doll or a puppet. A sort of gnome dressed as a woman. It took her some time to understand that it was her. And when she finally understood, the terror was so great that she started to run. The expanding effect of the house multiplied, then, and the woman soon saw herself disappear.

The music woke her. It was barely a whisper that came out of some speaker she couldn't see from the bed. A saxophone. A piano. Somewhere between the two. She got up, exasperated. She pressed various buttons on the dresser, but nothing changed. Then she picked up the phone to complain. The receptionist explained that it was the morning music.

"The morning music?" she repeated.

"Indeed," he said without getting upset.

"But I don't want to hear your morning music," she said, carefully enunciating each word.

"There isn't anything we can do from here," the man answered. "They're the morning exercises."

Furious, the journalist hung up and opened the curtains of the window that looked out on the street: pedestrians and lines of traffic. The anemic light of a winter sun. The whole day ahead. When she turned toward the window that looked out on a large interior patio, she was surprised to see a group of young men holding books in their hands. They were walking and reading at the same time. They gave the impression of being monks or eunuchs or beings that belonged to another world. She wanted to take a photograph but reconsidered: impossible to know if that was allowed or not. Then she changed her mind. She went to her suitcase and, after furiously searching it, had to admit she hadn't brought the camera. It wasn't that bad, she repeated to herself, but she couldn't stop the tears. She sat on the toilet and covered her face with both hands. She didn't know what she was doing there, spying on a procession of readers through the window of a city where she had never wanted to go. She didn't know what that smell was that drilled into her nose. She didn't know whether she would have to do another three or four interviews only to hear the same thing she'd heard the day before. She felt far away from everything that was her world, and that separation filled her with anxiety. And what if she couldn't go back, like the other two or three journalists, about whom nothing seemed to be known? And what if something happened to her in this place? The silent tears streaming down her cheeks now turned to sobs. Her chest burned. She felt a singular pressure on her sternum. Soon she wouldn't be able to breathe, and this idea didn't seem that absurd to her. She went on that way for a long time: thinking about absurd things. Then she inhaled. Then she exhaled. The sobs slowed. Finally, when she no longer remembered exactly what had brought her to the toilet, she said to herself: it's only six more days. She noticed that the morning music, as the receptionist had called it, had stopped. And she immediately started to bathe.

The reports that the Editor-in-Chief received sometime later read: "There was something in the hotel room, my body sensed that before my head. Something was stealthily, almost imperceptibly moving things out of place. I had refused to accept that it could be happening, which is perhaps why I refused to complain to reception, even though the stench was increasing day by day. But on the fourth day, right after I came back from conducting the scheduled interviews, I saw it. *To see* is a verb that could lend itself to misunderstandings here. I perceived something with my eyes. A movement or a glimmer crossed my line of vision. I didn't distinguish the contours or details of what I assumed, from the beginning, would be a face, a body, a pair of hands, legs. I had opened the closet doors unexpectedly, and the thing, whatever it was, couldn't hide quickly enough. I saw it. I perceived it. The presence was hiding in the back of the closet, taking shelter behind the clothes and emitting a strange purr. At first I thought it was a groan. Then I imagined it was a whine. In any case I closed the closet doors and, without taking my fingers from the handle, stood immobile for a long time."

She looked for the boy who had told her about the two or three journalists who'd stayed longer than planned. When she couldn't find him anywhere, she decided to wait for him in her room. She ordered some dinner and, upon opening the door, was happy to see his face.

"And where did they stay?" she asked, without waiting for the boy to remove the stainless-steel covers from the serving plates.

"Where did who stay?" His question was sincere.

"The journalists," she whispered, without being able to look him in the face. "The journalists you mentioned a few days ago."

"Oh, them," he said, and fell silent. Then he turned his back on her to continue serving the dinner. It was easy to imagine wings there, emerging from the shoulder blades of that wide, agile back. "No one knew," he muttered after a moment.

The journalist had always been able to distinguish truth from lies in the voices of her interviewees. She couldn't explain exactly what it was, but something, a certain timbre or tremor or tone, put her on alert. It almost never failed.

"The forest is close," whispered the boy without turning to look at her. "When someone wants to hide, they usually go there. To the forest."

She approached him. Pulled his elbow. Forced him to face her. The masculine face, with fine features and defined brows, had changed. He was no longer a boy but a man filled with terror. Or a caged animal. He had aged. He was about to collapse. A statue of stale bread. Monument of sand.

"And why would those two or three journalists you mentioned want to hide?"

Some of the reports the Editor-in-Chief received in the mail were accompanied by newspaper clippings. Stapled to blank pages or glued on with Elmer's were yellowing notes in which, years ago, someone had documented the sudden appearance of a wild being in the city. Not speaking their language and hunched over, the figure seemed to come from far away. From a place beyond time. A place without human context. No one knew if she'd been born there or if she'd been brought, later, to this tropical space. The doctors who examined her couldn't confirm she wasn't suffering from brain damage. They couldn't say, or didn't want to say, whether the scars around her wrists were signs of an unsuccessful suicide attempt or marks left behind from years in bondage. The truth is that, for all their efforts, which seem to have taken months if not years, the figure never recovered speech or verticality. In photographs, she sometimes gives the impression of being a woman, especially in the ones where long, black, tangled hair covers her face, revealing just a pair of thick parted lips. In others, however, she looks like a man: a young man who has been captured unsuspecting on film while imitating an ape. In yet others she is unrecognizable. La Inhumana, they called her from the beginning, conserving the feminine pronoun. La Inhumana arrived one day, without warning, and stayed all the years it took her to die. She periodically lived in a hospital for the chronically ill located on the outskirts of the city. One of the photographs showed the window through which the ineffable face looked out on something else, something unseen.

"You have to come with me," whispered the waiter as he placed his hand on her elbow and, gently pulling, led her from her room. "Trust me," he managed to whisper as he placed a blindfold over her eyes and pushed her inside a car whose motor was already running.

She was never sure how long the journey had taken. Upon recounting the events, she realized that sometimes she believed she had spent hours like that, not seeing anything, nauseated from the sudden swerves of the vehicle, only to later convince herself that it had been nothing more than a quick trip in concentric circles. The back seat was upholstered in a material soft to the touch, like velvet, but it smelled like piss and humidity. The air that entered through the open windows was warm and dense, something you could almost chew.

"Where are you taking me?" she asked with a calm that she felt without any apparent reason.

"Be quiet, please," was all she heard in response. Then the boy lit a cigarette and the smell of tobacco captivated her. A music she imagined as vespertine filled the car's air.

Everything happened quickly once they reached their destination. The boy opened the door and, with utmost care, removed the blindfold from her eyes. Then, with the same movement on her right elbow and still in silence, he urged her to walk down a dirt path that seemed to disappear under the battering of enormous green fronds. Mosquitos soon began to leave their red marks on her forearms. Finally, when she was prepared for anything, she saw a little hut with open doors and windows.

"Go in," the man urged her. "They're waiting for you."

The report that most caught the Editor-in-Chief's attention arrived in a separate package, half hidden between the dirty pages of some books. The smell of tobacco and, what else?, on his fingertips. He touched the pages with a certain melancholic sensation: her fingers, after all, had been there, the open palm of her hand, her eyes, the tips of her hair.

It said: "On the outskirts of order grows, with great stubbornness, another order. It isn't an alternative city, exactly, but a series of anti-cities that, scattered across the narrow borders, survive in constant motion. Founded and abandoned almost simultaneously, these hamlets can exist only if they aren't detected by the city's various surveillance systems. Going unnoticed is, then, their principal objective.

"There, in one of those ephemeral villages, the two or three journalists that didn't manage to leave the City of Men survive.

"They had been sent, like me, to write a series of reports about the peculiar city from a female point of view. And, after a couple days, they had realized, like me, that they would not be able to leave. Explaining that kind of thing tends to take an entire lifetime. When I found them in the hut that would soon disappear, they spoke to me swiftly as they joined hands. They said, almost in unison, without looking away from one another for a single moment: 'One cannot explain this kind of thing.' Then they offered me a warm drink, as warm as the rain that started falling over the forest.

"'The winters are very mild here,' one of them said, turning her back to me, looking at something outside the window.

"'If you're patient, soon enough something will grow,' said the other, pricking up her ear, as if the process could be detected from there.

"It took very little time for me to realize the obvious: the ex-journalists no longer understood my questions and I was incapable of understanding their answers. If anyone besides the hotel waiter had witnessed the exchange, they would have thought it a strange theatrical exercise.

"'Are you fleeing?' I asked.

"'From what?' they asked in unison, intrigued.

"'How did you decide to stay here?' I continued.

"'One never decides that kind of thing,' stammered one of them, the one who hadn't left her position by the window. 'That kind of thing happens. That. Happens. And then it stops happening.'

"'But something must have happened,' I insisted. 'Something must have precipitated this that happens and that, later, eventually, will stop happening.'"

"The ex-journalists looked at each other out of the corners of their eyes and then, with a sort of telepathic compassion, looked at me again.

"'Surely,' one of them whispered, 'something must have happened. Yes.'"

They lost contact with her almost the moment she left. The Editor-in-Chief found it strange not to receive any information about her arrival, and he didn't stop feeling a growing regret, a suspicion that little by little pressed on his chest as the days passed without any report on the City of Men from a woman's perspective. He imagined the worst, of course. On an optimistic day he thought the journalist might not have gotten on the plane and that she could be found, somewhat fearful but rebellious, in her apartment, and he went there. He knocked on the door, anxious. Then he knocked on the door irritated, convinced she was in there, hunkered down. When the doorman agreed to open it, they had to cover their nose: the cat had died. The morning dust floated over the furniture, simply there. Still in disbelief, the Editor-in-

Chief went to the study. He ran his fingers over the spines of some books. He touched the computer keyboard. Then, without knowing why, he walked toward the window and covered his face with both hands. The person who saw him crying from the window across the street was left suddenly paralyzed: she too felt a slight pressure on her chest. She looked at the sun. The reflections of the morning sun on the glass. And she held her hand to her heart that didn't stop beating rapidly, very rapidly.

Once on his way back to his office, the Editor-in-Chief made a few calls, sent messages by fax and email. He thought for a moment about placing a small note in the international section noting the journalist's departure date and the last time anyone had heard from her. After much hesitation, he decided to wait a few more days. He didn't want to cause panic among the employees or diplomatic missteps between the two cities. He remained silent. He drank coffee. The weight on his chest impeded him from sleeping, digesting food, picturing himself with her.

She went to the Hospital for the Chronically Ill the morning of her seventh day in the City of Men. The sky was gray and a warm rain, a rain so warm it felt like tea, coated her hair. No one stopped her from walking through the lobby and, when she ordered a taxi, the car appeared all at once. As soon as she closed the door, she noticed the red velvet seat and, with her open palm on it, looked for the driver in the rearview mirror. The man's eyes found hers and, seconds later, without any change on his delicate, masculine features, looked away. A warm wind, dense and aromatic at once, made its way through her mouth until it arrived, softly, in her lungs. She felt alive. She was about to say so. She was about to say: I am alive. But she held back.

The hospital was majestic. The façade of austere vertical lines, high security, of historical significance. On a hill, surrounded by tall stone walls, the hospital gave the impression of being on top of itself. A building suspended in air. A pure ascension. The journalist climbed the central staircase. When she reached the top, someone was already waiting for her. A man in a white robe stretched out his hand and invited her in.

"The director is busy right now, but he won't be long."

She nodded and, once alone inside the main office, started sniffing around the books on the shelves and looking out windows at the landscape surrounding the building.

"The forest doesn't look like a forest from here, don't you think?" said the man with salt-and-pepper hair as soon as he entered the office, before extending his right hand to her.

"Indeed," she said, deep in thought.

"You will recognize the smell," he continued as he straightened some papers on the desk. "One always ends up recognizing that smell wherever one goes."

The journalist held her breath and, at the same time, without noticing she was doing it, moved her right hand toward her chest. The pressure there. The desire to run away. A weight.

"The cemetery is over there; can you see it?" asked the Director, walking up behind her. His index finger erect. Something unidentifiable on the other side of the window. "The crypts always disappear under the smothering plants. I suppose that's the good thing about having a cemetery in the forest," he concluded.

The journalist walked by his side as they toured the different wards of the institution. Nothing of what she saw there surprised her. The Director moved slowly down the empty hallways as if he had no other commitment that day. Calm, with a modulated, friendly voice, he described to her the kinds of ailments they treated as well as the quality of the cornices.

"Look," he pointed to the stained-glass windows. "A true relic. Truly beautiful."

The journalist nodded. She took notes. When she finally arrived in the patients' ward, she remained silent. It was what she expected to find, certainly. It was what her imagination had previously given her: a swift accumulation of misfortunes, a series of lethal injuries, mortification in plural. She looked at their faces and, rather than feel compassion, thought she might vomit. She tried to recognize something human in all of it, but when she realized that was impossible, she had to lean on a handrail. What kind of monster was she that couldn't even look the patients in the eye? It was there, one step from the abyss, that she became aware of her utter loneliness. Between the incessant noise and the smell of something corrupt and the hands that extended toward her body, the journalist felt a faint fear and, because of that fear, turned to seek out the Director. She had no idea how to return to the Main Office, and her anxiety at such a discovery forced her to walk more quickly, with no concern about bumping into other bodies or even brusquely pushing them aside. She opened doors, pulled back curtains, looked for signs. She had the urgent sensation that she had very little time. She needed protection. She wanted a place to take shelter.

"This is always what happens the first time," the Director said when he saw her enter his spacious office. A soft boredom in the voice.

"Look," he said without waiting for the journalist to catch her breath or calm down. He opened a tiny door to his left and, after turning on the light, invited her in. The journalist hesitated, but quickly understood it was an order. The narrowness of the space forced her to brush against him when she passed. It was the same smell. It was the smell that, according to him, always ended up being recognized. Everywhere. Always.

He'd made few decisions while waiting. He still didn't want to provoke a diplomatic conflict, yet he couldn't simply sit there doing nothing. For all he knew, the journalist he'd sent off to the City of Men could have been dead already. He talked with a couple of friends about what had happened. One remembered the case of the two or three journalists, he wasn't sure how many, who'd gone to the peculiar city and never returned.

"The rumor was," he said, somewhat mockingly, "they ended up finding husbands."

The Editor-in-Chief didn't join in the laughter around the table. With a preoccupied scowl, he asked for more. He wanted details, dates, names. Had anyone looked for them? For how long before giving up?

The answers made him remember a dream. He was waiting next to a telephone booth. When the telephone finally rang, he realized he was muzzled. He couldn't feel his mouth. He couldn't talk. There he was, the receiver before his face, and he couldn't talk.

The car that would take her to the airport arrived on time the night of her seventh day in the City of Men. The journalist had packed her belongings carefully, delicately folding her clothes and taking care not to forget anything in the bathroom. Then she ordered a light dinner to her room. The waiter who brought up the tray didn't try to start a conversation, disappearing as soon as he uncovered the salad and uncorked a little bottle of wine. The journalist, who sat waiting, poured the contents into a cup and drank it in sips. Through the window she could see the rain, the gray sky, the looming storm clouds. She had a sudden desire to stick her head out the window and open her mouth to prove that it wasn't actually tea. She smiled when she thought about that.

At the agreed upon hour, reception let her know a car was waiting. A young boy helped her with the bags, and another opened the door while she avoided looking back. The driver met her gaze in the rearview mirror and, without talking, took off.

The report that the Editor-in-Chief would eventually receive and read, while sitting by the phone, recounted:

"The light was visceral that day. It was not the light we know as twilight, nor the violent eruption of morning lightning. This light was something else: the light of a cloudy day. The light trying to be light, without fully achieving it, failing." He paused his reading, cleared his throat. He looked out the window. He had the impression that the telephone would ring at any moment. "I knew what they had planned for me because it was what had happened to the two or three previous journalists: on the way to the airport, as I closed my eyes, relieved after seven days of anxiety and work, an accident would force the driver to change his route. That is precisely what happened. The car left the highways and went down smaller, unpaved streets. When we went into the forest it started to get dark, but the light, that thin winter light, still filtered through the evening cracks. That is what I paid attention to, to avoid the panic. The light saved me.

"I assumed that he would abandon me at the edge of the trail at any moment. That was his strategy: open the door and deposit me at the beginning of nothingness. An incommensurable and green everything. Time would take care of everything else. Time would take care of all else. Meanwhile, I write. Meanwhile, I take shelter in this hut and write. Soon those who found the cities and then abandon them will arrive. Soon I will have to run away from here. Meanwhile: I write. Meanwhile, I understand that I write."

He paused his reading again. He watched the telephone, silent. He poured himself a little liquor in a large glass.

"Soon, too, I will stop understanding. When someone snatches this piece of paper from my hands, I will no longer understand."

The Last Sign

The whirlwind came out of nowhere. They were slowly walking across the median strip when the leaves from the trees suddenly started to swirl into the air along with newspaper pages and plastic bottles. The dust forced him to close his eyes and, almost immediately, to grab onto the thin trunk of a poplar tree. An embrace. Some time later, one of the pedestrians who saw the spectacle from the sidewalk would say in his testimony that the image of the man embracing the tree had seemed beautiful to him: he was carrying his briefcase in one hand and his tie, skinny and blue, was flying up toward the sky along with his hair. He would add: there was a kind of abandonment in it. A desire to stay. Something of a shipwreck.

The pedestrian, who spoke like a poet, wouldn't say anything about the woman.

As soon as he opened his eyes, the Man from the Tree looked for her. He was smiling in anticipation of their reunion, wanting to share something someone had told him as a child, that whirlwinds of that kind—sudden, slender, violent—meant the devil was close by. He hoped she would open her mouth and then pull from her lungs, from the humid insides of her body, that funny, true laughter that so pleased him. He imagined she would take him by the hand and, still laughing, even shaking her head, lead him away from there. They would walk together, he thought. But he lost her.

He assumed the whirlwind had scared her and that, coming from so far away and unaccustomed to that particular climatic phenomena, she might have sought refuge somewhere. He was tempted to believe that, disoriented by the violence of the wind, she'd found shelter in some nearby doorway. He hoped he might find her in the shop next door, squinting at records. In passing, he imagined that the whirlwind might have lifted her up by the waist and taken her to the devil's house. He smiled again and headed home with untroubled steps.

When he called her the first time, he thought that even though she didn't answer, she was there, her hands under running water washing a plate, two cups, a spoon. He'd always liked her carefulness, that way she moved among the objects of the world as if they were about to break or about to hurt her. How her voice fluctuated. The way she lowered her gaze before praise, flirtation, or shame. Her faint footsteps over the floorboards. When he dialed her number the second time, he imagined her waist and the devil's arms around it. He looked up at the night sky: two creatures tangled like threads of smoke. Vanishing. He drank the green tea she had brought to his house in a little tin can. She had shown him the correct way to prepare and drink it. He pronounced her name. He said: Xian. Then he picked up the phone again. It was past midnight when he started to worry.

He would emphatically tell the Detective in charge of this case that he hadn't noticed anything strange about the woman's behavior the day of the whirlwind. He'd met her at their usual restaurant—a small, unpretentious establishment that served complex, delicately flavored dishes that had quickly won their enthusiastic devotion. Between mouthfuls they'd talked, as usual, about stuff. The climate. The traffic. The flavor of pepper or cloves. The aftertaste of the garlic. Then after the coffee they had decided to walk back, something else they frequently did. He held his briefcase; she, her handbag. They crossed the avenue, and it was there, right in the median strip with the poplar trees, that the whirlwind formed, sudden and out of nowhere. He closed his eyes and, out of instinct, managed to get close to something that seconds later he realized was the trunk of a tree. He assumed the woman had done the same.

"Did you know," the Detective would ask, hiding her eyes in a cup of coffee, "that on that same day, in the province of Hunan, someone related to your friend died?"

"Yan Huanyi?" he'd ask in turn, incredulous.

"That's it," she'd reply, handing over a thin, yellowing piece of paper that looked, and this also seemed incredible to him, like a telegram.

"I didn't think anyone used these anymore," he'd murmur with the paper still in his hands. "Telegraphs, I mean. This communication system," he would stop short, ashamed, because he couldn't believe that while thinking about Xian's disappearance his mind could also be occupied by such a banal and distant matter.

The Detective would lower her gaze and the Man from the Tree wouldn't be able to ignore the parallel: it was the same timid, secretive gesture that, in his version of the world, belonged to Xian. A gesture that could hardly go unnoticed, especially in a working woman. An ancient expression that, in his imagination, came from far away, from a world about to disappear. That was Xian for him, he would realize: a far-off world in the process of extinction. A species in danger. Except that now Xian had indeed disappeared. Now Xian had fulfilled her unspoken promise.

"Anything you remember could be very helpful for us," the Detective would say, standing up and handing him her card. Then she'd shake his hand and quickly cross the avenue.

The only thing he'd remember while he watched her disappear among the other pedestrians under the sticky afternoon light was the sound of the whirlwind in his ears. A faint tremor. A sharp whistle. The sonorous crash of trivial things. A dance of discarded items. And further back, once the fear had found its place in his stomach, the beating of his heart, the grinding of his teeth. The confluence of enamel and dust and saliva. A form of abrasion. True torture. He'd remember himself, many years before, in another place. He'd remember the period of dust storms and the way he clung to lampposts imagining the worst: to be carried off by the wind. He'd remember the wide avenues across which dried grass, tricycles, all kinds of trash bounced. The fear would return with the gesture: the hand that latches onto something before the undefined possibility of separation. Before the possibility of being left alone. Before this.

"Xian," he'd say out loud to no one, "Xian is a strange woman."

Then he would slowly head home.

Days later, Xian's neighbor said in his testimony that he saw the man in front of her door late one night through his peephole. He recognized him, of course. He'd seen him many times. The Man in Front of the Door pulled a set of keys from his jacket pocket, put one of them in the lock, and let himself in. He described him as a taciturn, tired man. Silent. He said that, judging by the absence of noise, the man hadn't done anything, simply let himself fall into the living room armchair, an apricot-red chair that to the neighbor had always looked comfortable but was also beautiful. Perhaps he'd occupied himself staring at the ceiling, or perhaps he'd just fallen asleep. The neighbor quietly repeated: let himself fall. This is what he imagined he had done. And that, of course, had seemed suspicious.

He didn't know why he made the decision to walk toward Xian's house instead of heading home. Maybe the wind. Maybe a sudden nostalgia. He opened the door with his set of keys and entered. He didn't know exactly how long he was there, but it was already dark, the darkest point of the night, when he left carrying one of her handkerchiefs in the right pocket of his shirt, close to his body, against his chest, where only someone looking for it would have found it.

The Man Who Was Afraid of Whirlwinds would have known that Nüshu is a secret language. Or was. That the women of Hunan province had created it in the third century, and since then had passed it on from generation to generation like a scandalous female secret. He would know everything Xian had told him about that women's writing: that it was a form of expression in an oppressively masculine environment; that it was inscribed on paper or painted on fans or stitched onto handkerchiefs; that it was used to compose the so-called Third Day Missives with which friends and family members sent advice to a newlywed. To the woman who has gone away. He would know that Nüshu consisted of fine, slender lines—lines he found enchanting. He would know, finally, about the vast distance between the province of Hunan and the terracotta soldiers of Xian and, because of that, he wouldn't have believed anything Xian told him. That's why he would have let her talk.

The pedestrian who, some time later, gave his testimony, insisted that he never saw any woman there, next to the Man Embracing a Tree. He emphatically said: there was no woman there. I am sure of that.

The neighbor, who days later remembered something he thought might be useful, called to say that he forgot to mention the whispers. He said that he hadn't immediately noticed them. That he only learned about the whispers when he stopped hearing them. Conspicuous in their absence. He said that, now that he remembered, he knew the whispers began punctually in the evenings and it wasn't unusual for them to continue into the night. Sometimes they would even wake him up in the early morning. He corrected himself: he wasn't woken up by the whispers, which, naturally, were very quiet. He was woken up by the cold or the sudden movement of his wife's feet under the covers or the spasm of some nightmare. Once awake, he heard them. Once he had been awake for several minutes, when the night returned to its previous rhythm, when he had already spent time staring at the ceiling, then he heard them. Two voices intertwined. Two voices like two bodies of an indescribable softness. A lullaby. A prayer. Something that rocked him back to sleep and returned him, soundly, to his dream.

I would like for this story to take place in a far-off province, in a little village covered in gray and white storm clouds. A humid day. That was the beginning of the diary, which, hours later, would be included as evidence in the case called the Disappearance of the Woman in a Whirlwind. *I would like for you to be a woman from China.*

He always liked Chinese women. Their fragile wrists. Their smooth hair. Their light brown eyes. Their delicate frames. When he entered her, he liked to imagine he could pierce through her.

He liked to imagine that it was only a question of time before he thrust right through her. The images were these: a butterfly pinned to a corkboard. A perforated insect on a sparkling clean laboratory bench. A bead strung together with another: bursts of color. The Man Who Was Afraid of Whirlwinds didn't tell the Detective about any of that. She would gather that information days later, as she read the diary with the reddish-orange satin cover she kept, against the rules, hidden away in her desk drawer. Not only was the Detective intrigued by the two different handwritings contained in the notebook, she also found the object itself beautiful. It was obvious that the diary, which told a story that one of the two lovers imagined happening somewhere else, a far-off humid place, was something more than just a receptacle for their longing. After her first reading, a hurried reading full of curiosity, a reading that was more like a process of digestion, the Detective would become obsessed by the idea that the diary in which their desires were inscribed was, in turn, a source of new desires. A sort of engine. A machine. Increasingly explicit desires. Desires of fusion. Increasingly exact desires. Pointed desires. Desires that would keep her reading the diary throughout the day and sometimes the night, entering the space of the pages with their cherry-colored tint whose density and aroma reminded her of the bouquet of a fine wine. Seated with the diary, greedily reading it on the messy surface of her desk, the Detective would look like she was eating. In place of food, this was how the Detective nourished herself.

A few days later, after the inhabitants of the city began gossiping about what had happened, the afternoon newspaper would express it this way: MYSTERIOUS WHIRLWIND. WOMAN FROM CHINA DISAPPEARS.

Carve your back. Mark your back. Cut furrows in the skin of your back. Bite your back. Climb up on your back. Pierce your back. Watch the red drop slide down your back. Suck your back. Provoke your back. Lie on your back.

The signs carved marked open on my back. The signs that are holes on my back that is your back. Sucked provoked resting, the back. A dune. A valley. An undulation. The spine. Spi(k)e. S(h)ine.

Weeks later, the woman who cleaned Xian's apartment said in an accented Spanish that she had personally hand-washed the blood-stained sheets in the stone basin behind the kitchen. It was an exhausting chore that frequently took her multiple hours. She used lavender soap. She said she liked to breathe in the smell of the sheets afterward, once they were hanging from the clothesline up on the rooftop. Their shadows like a slow dance among ghosts. She said it wasn't until then that she wondered what had happened on them, on the sheets. What those stains, those bitter rancid smells meant. Those traces. She never found the answer. She never asked the question out loud.

Touch your thigh. Macerate your thigh. Grind your thigh. Mark it like you mark dead skin.

The heat of the iron. The strength of the iron. The inscription. The scream. The sudden inhalation. The exhalation that shudders.

Touch my thigh. Mark my thigh. Grind my thigh. Mark it like you mark dead skin. Revive it.

The thigh. The exile.

There are two kinds of handwriting, the Detective would later explain to the Young Policeman who was looking at her attentively from the doorway. Feet crossed. Black shoes. Tight pants over the thighs. These were two scripts, certainly, but it was impossible to know which belonged to the man, which belonged to the woman. It was impossible to know who did what to whom, who let what be done, who desired, who desired more.

"Explain that to me," the Young Policeman would answer, intrigued and immobile. Statue on the threshold. Notions of Rome.

"It's the subject," she'd mutter in response, squinting her eyes. "It must be the subject," she would repeat. Then, talking more to herself than to him, she would add:

"I never know who the subject of the sentence is."

"Ah, that," he'd murmur. "A sentence."

Many years later, the Man Who Swore He Had Lost a Woman from China wondered why he had chosen to get a tattoo right around that time. More than once, especially when it rained, as he watched the evening rain behind a window, he wondered why he had chosen those very days, when the Detective and the Young Policeman were investigating the case with what seemed, from the start, a frenzied passion, to place that seemingly arbitrary sign just below his left earlobe.

Seconds after spotting the four-leaf clover behind his ear, the Detective would furrow her brow and think that she didn't really know anything about the Man Who Was in Front of Her. He seemed normal—the striped shirt made him seem so—but she was aware that appearances tend to be an entryway and not necessarily an exit. And there was a dark tunnel between the two.

"And that?" She couldn't avoid asking, pointing to the left side of his neck with feigned carelessness.

Instinctively bringing his hand to the back of his neck, the man would smile and remain silent. Looking at her directly, suddenly still. The Detective, accustomed to deciphering unexpected behaviors, would know the man really didn't know what to say. The Man Who Was in Front of Her was surely a Man without Answers.

In the moment of selecting the design, he thought about the southern seas and heard, in that instant, the word *incommensurable*. An echo. Two. He heard the word *ta-tau: mark on the skin*. He thought about Polynesia. He thought about the Maoris, for whom tattooing the face was a sign of social distinction. Somewhere in his mind he wrote the signs XVIII, knowing they meant *the eighteenth century*. He pictured the ships that carried and returned James

Cook, and he desired, with a desire as incommensurable as the one that had evoked the southern seas, to go there: to go on a ship. To let himself be taken away.

Mark yourself on me. Mark yourself in me. Mark me with you. Open the skin; cut the skin; penetrate the epidermis: introduce the ink.

Mark yourself with ink: masticate yourself, mince yourself, mash yourself. Swallow yourself.

Define yourself with ink. Bind yourself.

Facing another whirlwind, the Man Who Swore He Had Lost a Woman from China wondered, a year later, if any of it had really happened. He remembered it as if from a distance, as if looking through a car window. The devil, he'd say to himself. And then he'd press the gas and avoid looking at the dust cloud in his rearview mirror.

Once public attention waned in the case of the Woman Who Disappeared Behind a Whirlwind, the Detective would picture the two of them lying on a satin bed, their calves just peeking out from the edge of the eiderdown, dictating entire paragraphs to one another. One morning. Her image of the scene would be so intense that, even after climbing into her car, turning it on, and moving through the streets of the city, she would still smell their bodies: a mixture of semen and ink and sweat and wine. Pressing the brake before a stoplight, she would smell a combination of desire and sentence. Their sentence. And in that moment, she would have to admit it: the Detective desired them. She wanted to be one of them. She wanted to be there, in the bed. She wanted to be part of the event. To be marked in that violent and sagacious, ludic, infantile way. That's why she kept reading: *I would like for you to be from China. I want you to stick in my smooth-mouthed nakedness: a knife. I want the burning of the blow and the slow agony of the laceration. The pin. The nail. The clamp. I want the letter.* Later she'd think this morning vision—seemingly incongruent, seemingly gratuitous—of their bodies on the satin bed was tied to the image of a hummingbird suspended over an open flower, whose wingbeat had anguished her earlier, at dawn. The incessant wingbeat. A man and a woman on a satin bed: the desperate wingbeat: a man and a woman who write words of mutual harm: the irremediable wingbeat: a man and a woman dictating to each other their sorrow, their plea, their hope. The wingbeat. Only thus could you explain, she would tell the Young Policeman a little later that same day, the ambiguous authorship of each diary entry. That not-knowing. That darkness surrounding the grammatical subject. Only thus could you explain how the diary, the writing of the diary, simultaneously revealed their most intimate selves and masked them perfectly. Only thus could you explain the whispers. Those evenings. Those nights. And the ear of the insomniac neighbor on the wall next door.

You in place of me: I in your place.

Y-ours-elves: in that place. If you were from China.

A humid place: y-ours.

"But that isn't a clover!" she'd murmur, astonished, in the early morning, at the beginning or end of one of those fateful days, when she still believed she could solve the case, when she imagined that the case of the Woman Who Disappeared in a Whirlwind had a solution. Her long fingers: with uniformly cut nails: on the figure etched into the man's skin. A sort of tremor. A long wait.

"Indeed," he'd answer, half asleep but still alert. "This isn't a clover," and in that moment, just as he finished the phrase, he'd turn to look at her: his mouth open, his hair tangled, the terrible waiting. The Detective—he wouldn't realize this until then—was a woman as tense as a mandolin string, with the barely concealed curvature of a tall palm tree, prisoner of a strange mental life. In front of her, in front of that bundle of nerves—the Tense Woman, the Woman About to Break Down—he'd have an immense desire to pronounce the words southern-seas, Ta-tau, Maoris, but he wouldn't do it.

"It's a Nüshu word," he'd whisper close to her ear, "Guanyin," he'd pull back and look her in the face again, enjoying the way the Detective suffered in the waiting. "The name of a Buddhist goddess."

"The last character?" she'd then ask, winking her left eye. A blow when it's returned. The silence and, within the silence, the blow that bursts onto the Tattooed Man's cheekbone. The noise of the blow and, within the noise of the blow, the dry sound of the head that crashes against the tiles.

"And her name really was Xian?" she'd inquire still later: the body of the man on the satin sheets: the hummingbird suspended on the other side of the window: the Vengeful Woman who leaves.

The pedestrian who provided his testimony over and over would say again, each time with the same firmness, that he hadn't seen any woman there, in the vicinity of the median strip. No woman, he repeated. There wasn't any woman whatsoever.

The Young Policeman would tell her, the penultimate point of the day's report, that according to his quick research on Nüshu, it had indeed existed and it had indeed disappeared. It was a sort of secret code produced by women in the province of Hunan that, from the third century on, was passed from generation to generation. He'd then show her a sheet that compared Nüshu characters and Chinese characters, with which the Detective would be able to confirm that the first were square and the second cursive and slender. The Young Policeman would then tell her that not only could Nüshu be found on scrolls, but also on handkerchiefs, fans, clothes. Domestic objects. Household things.

"Or on the skin," the Tense Woman would mutter to herself as, ashamed by her earlier outburst, suddenly blushing, she would lower her gaze. That gesture.

The Young Policeman would then add, with a compassion she

could not fail to notice, that the Mandarin language, as a funda-
mental institution of Chinese culture, had an authoritarian, hier-
archical, and solemn structure while Nüshu was for women the
language of daily life, of emotions, of spontaneity, of the natural
world, of dreams, and of desires.

Then, before turning around, he would mention almost ran-
domly that, for that reason, women tended to use Nüshu to write
the Third Day Missives, pamphlets written on fabric in which
women transmitted marriage advice to their daughters. These
letters were sent to brides on the third day after their wedding. To
the women who had gone away.

They talked about it, he remembered much later. After the selection of the design, after leaving the tattoo parlor, after the curious eye of the Detective noticed it behind his ear, even after she
asked him if Xian really was her name. The name of the Woman
Who Disappeared Behind a Whirlwind. He remembered it on an
afternoon like any other, in his car. An afternoon of out-of-sync
traffic lights. Thin clouds. Smoke everywhere. He remembered
that they'd talked about it, the tattoo. About it being the last word.
This mark that would come to signify, in the future, in an unimaginable future, the word *end*. The event.

"The end of writing," he'd whispered then, his right hand on
the woman's pink nipple, the jasmine-scented lips on his neck.

"The end of this." One of the two had said it. This.

One day, when he began to forget her, when he even started to
wonder whether her name had really been Xian, the Man Who

Was Afraid of Whirlwinds entered an unfamiliar café. Having walked without a fixed destination, at a normal speed—yet filled with anguish—under the afternoon glare. Having walked without stopping only to find himself, as night approached, empty, indifferent, thirsty. He would push open the swinging doors and approach the bar. He ordered the first thing the waiter, a man with a prominent belly and black vest, offered him: a glass of thick liquid, crowned with foam. He stayed silent, avoiding eye contact with the other diners, examining the tip of his right shoe, the stains on the big, beveled mirror, the reflection of the room, the corner farthest from the ceiling. He would have spent hours that way, motionless, alone. He would have sat that way until another man appeared, just as tired as he was. Just as hunched over. Just as evasive. The Man Who Swore to Have Lost a Woman from China recognized himself in this new arrival, the Parsimonious Man Who Blocked the View, and so in asking him, "Are you also terrified to go home?" he thought he was asking himself. Something strange, something dark, something perhaps trivial and perhaps unnamable would have compelled the Hunched Man, the Evasive Man, to come out of his silence, hissing, "What scares me is my head."

"Do you imagine terrible things?" the other man then asked, with the interest that can only be sparked by difference. The end of identification.

The Evasive Man lowered his gaze (that gesture) and hid himself for a while in the silence that answered the question. His arms crossed over his chest as if he were cold.

"I imagine," he said after drinking three or four sips of his viscous drink, advancing and stopping short a couple times, opening and closing his mouth without managing to say anything. "I imagine I'm killing a woman, for example," his voice almost inaudible at the end of the sentence.

"Do you imagine you cover her mouth her eyes her breasts? Do you imagine your hands squeezing destroying clawing squeezing more? The blood draining, drop by drop, do you imagine it? Do you imagine yourself pushing through her slitting her open fragmenting her? Do you imagine the last breath?"

"I imagine that the woman disappears behind a whirlwind, one afternoon," he murmured with his eyes on his drink. "I imagine that."

Another pedestrian swore in his statement that there had been a woman there, in the whirlwind. He said that the image was memorable for him because it was the face of someone who had come too far. He corrected himself immediately, adding: it was the face of a woman who had come too far and who was nevertheless ready to go even farther. She was preparing for that. A long journey.

He said he hadn't said anything before because no one had asked him.

Sometime later, when she was trying to solve one of the most difficult cases of her career, the case of the Castrated Men, in moments when the Detective was about to move her hand, her fingertips, toward a mark on the body of another suspect, she would suddenly remember everything. She'd experience the yearning.

That atrocious cloud. That stab. The sound that, like the gale of wind, makes the sounds of the body audible. That buried exclamation point. That bursting. And she'd then remember the puzzling tattoo on the neck of the Man Who Swore He Had Lost a Woman from China Behind a Whirlwind, that had forced her to lose herself. Inside. Inside herself. Outside. She'd remember the sensation of the split skin under her touch (the printed skin) (the stamped skin) and the dizziness, a subtle way of sliding nowhere, would envelope her again. The speed: a face that disappears and appears: a backlight: the skeins of air that, around her neck, her wrists, her waist, squeeze. And squeeze. She'd remember the satin bed, the frozen feet, the scarlet ink that slid over the thighs, the corners of the mouth, the shin. She'd remember the indentation of the tooth on the abdomen, the indent of the fingernails on the breasts, the hair knotted in the knuckles. She'd remember the staggered vision laid over Herself. An image behind another. Another image. A constant stabbing. How far can you go? She'd remember everything and then the hand turned into a fist would remain immobile in her pocket.

The furrows in your skin, open. Put me in there. Ink, hand, nail, yoke.

Write yourself. Truly write yourself. Sign, wedge, sharpen. Write yourself here: in y-our place.

Literally write yourself, ok?

—

Before, before everything, the Man Who Would Swear He Had Lost a Woman from China would stop in front of a whirlwind. He'd be afraid at first (a sort of dizziness) (a way of slipping nowhere) (that throb) and then, almost immediately, he'd remember that someone had told him, in his childhood, that that kind of whirlwind—slender, sudden, vertical—meant that the devil was close by. Then he'd see everything all at once: the devil, the body of the devil, the arms of the body of the devil, embracing the waist of a woman. A waltz. A strident melody of violins. Feet, levitating.

Offside

I would soon run out of gas, so when the battered sign appeared announcing a gas station ahead, I smiled. Ten kilometers. My agitated breath fogged up the windshield, but my hands, protected by thick wool gloves, were able to clear enough space to see the gray band of highway. An arrow in black.

Here.

The desolation of the gas station didn't surprise me so much as the scrawny face of the man on the other side of the dark counter, staring out at snowflakes whimsically floating through the air. His attitude made me pause before the window to watch the winter landscape, caught in the strange calm. For a moment I forgot my old car was there, immobile and waiting for the precious liquid. Forgot the cold. Forgot I had a long way left to go. It wasn't until a gust of wind rose, spinning a rusted weathervane, that I came back to reality.

"Gasoline," I murmured, too timidly, placing a handful of coins on the counter.

The man looked at the coins first and then at my face without any change of expression. He didn't seem to understand what was happening. I repeated the word and pointed to my car. In response, he emitted a series of unintelligible grunts and then went back to watching the snow with the same concentration as before. If I hadn't been so bewildered by his response, I might have found something pleasing in the way his gaze reached out to meet the snow. Something childlike. Something in perpetual levitation. Perhaps I noticed it. Perhaps I understood it. I cannot otherwise explain why I left that room so meekly and why I started walking toward the center of that town. One kilometer. A black arrow.

Here.

As soon as I entered the restaurant, I knew I was hungry. The smells were unrecognizable, but my stomach gurgled in anticipation of being filled. I sat down at one of the many free tables and immediately asked for the menu. The waitress who stopped at my side seemed annoyed by my request. She looked at me for what felt a long time, then, without saying a word, handed me two loose sheets of paper. But I couldn't decipher them, as hard as I tried.

"I'm sorry. I don't understand anything," I said. And she, who didn't seem to understand me either, headed toward the kitchen. Out came a tall, disheveled man who enunciated a wavering greeting as he dried his hands on his white apron.

"Foreign?" he asked. Blue eyes. Open eyes. Eyes that knew things.

I answered immediately that yes, I was indeed *foreign*. The word, a bit anachronistic, pleased me a great deal in that moment. I truly liked it. When he sat down at the table and started talking in the hesitating, slow way of someone not perfectly in control of the language, I realized this was the first true conversation I'd held in days. Before: hands on the wheel. Before: the interminable highway. Before: the humming of the engine. Before: the wide, white, terrible, winter silence. Before: nowhere.

"You won't be able to leave with this storm," he said, pointing outside, concerned. "Come," he added almost immediately, without waiting for an answer.

The sunlight had faded—I reconsidered too late. I was also slow to notice how quickly the footprints leading from the restaurant to the narrow door of his house vanished. Two hundred meters. No arrow in the color black. Here.

I slept many hours. Perhaps twenty-three. Maybe thirty-one. The first thing I saw when I woke up was the face of the man from the restaurant whose eyes gleamed at the word "foreign."

"Your car," he told me with a remorseful gesture. "Your car is gone."

The news didn't scare me. I neither asked how it had happened nor did I get upset. Instead, I remained silent. I closed my eyes again. I stretched under the white sheets. I flexed each of my toes. I assume the time passed. I opened my eyes again, observed him. Only then could I confirm, with a strange serenity, that the winter landscape on the other side of the window was the same.

That's how I met him. And that's how I agreed to stay. A black arrow. Here.

I soon learned that winter never left this place. The snow kept falling, sometimes lightly, sometimes tumultuously, but always white. Always. The cold limited my excursions and, on the rare occasions I accompanied him to the restaurant, my poor handling of their language made me awkward. I preferred to sit in front of the fire, looking out the window, letting time pass. I came to understand why the man at the gas station was so silent. Had I been able, I would have liked to talk to him. Talk for a long time. Talk about the hypnosis the falling snow provokes. In what I imagined was summertime in some other part of the world, the man from the restaurant and I had our first son. Two autumns later, the second was born. I accepted both with equal strength, with equal affection. In the moment of their birth, I insisted on placing their bloody bodies on my chest. Here. A red arrow. That warmth. When they were old enough to speak, I taught them my language.

"That's how I learned," their father said, accidentally interrupting one of our morning sessions. "My mother was a foreigner," he added, as if I already knew. Then he placed the tips of his fingers on my chin, which I took to mean he approved of my teaching.

Soon after, he started taking the children out without any notice, without any indication of where they were going. He asked only that I bundle them up and make a basket with provisions, filled water bottles and cleats. Then they would abruptly disappear only to reappear, days later, days that felt like entire weeks to me, with their cheeks reddened, their hair dirty, their legs covered in bruises, their faces crisscrossed with scratches. Once, one of them, the smaller one, came home missing a tooth.

I would hardly recognize them when they returned. They looked like another woman's children. They looked, in fact, like they didn't come from any woman. Their faces had that unintelligible and furious air of the nomads who, from time to time, would occupy the central plaza without anyone being able to do anything about it. They came, sold their leather goods, their iron tools, their seeds, and they left. There was something wild in their bright eyes, something determined in the way they picked up objects or breathed in the afternoon air. There was something powerful. Something like an echo. I moved among my own children as if they were strangers. As if they were the Nomads. When they ate around the fire, the boys would throw their arms in the air, screaming, bursting into laughter. I envied them that. Their gestures. The gleam in their faces. The sudden happiness. They only fell silent if they heard my footsteps or sensed, as they often did, that I was crouched behind the kitchen door, listening. If I suddenly appeared with a steaming pot of soup or with hot bread in my hands, they would change the tone of their voices. To talk about me they would use that universal term: "Ma." I, in such moments, only called them "the boys."

From the beginning I tried to learn where they went, what they did there, why they returned. I thought of questions I would later ask in intimate moments, such as before bed, when I'd bundle them up under eiderdown comforters, or during our language classes, when I knew no one else was listening to or understood us. Most of the time I settled for discretely spying on them, watching them out of the corner of my eye as they played on the patio, or walking at the same speed when they accompanied me to the market to buy vegetables. Nothing worked. They were as hermetic as their father. Their silence was like the snow: sometimes constant, sometimes flexible, but always white. Always falling like a subtle curtain between us. Always separating us.

A lot of time had passed when I tried to get information from the man at the gas station. I was out of my mind. I went to the gas station during one of their absences, one afternoon right before the storm began. I stood in front of him like the first time and, defeated once again by his concentrated attitude, I watched the falling snow in absolute silence by his side. The thin yellow light behind the flakes made me think that surely, in some other part of the world, it was winter once again.

"You're never going to accept it, are you?" the man asked me softly; a warm voice, in fact. When I realized I understood him, I sank into a sudden sadness, and my stupor kept me from saying anything in response.

"You should give up," he added, unbothered by my silence, and without lifting his deep gray eyes from the window's surface. "Why would you want to know?"

I was going to say that I had the right to know, that I wanted to know them, that they were part of my family. Mine. Of my body. I was going to say so many things, but I only managed to open my mouth. The condensation made me think that the world was nothing more than a great, steamed-up windshield, and this thought provoked in me a silent fit of tears.

"Look," the man said, pointing to a white hill barely visible through one of the window's corners. "Look," he insisted.

I dried my tears and looked. I saw it. I saw it all. I blew my nose and looked at him, holding my breath: he was the same, composed and comfortable behind the counter. He was a strange man, but he no longer scared me. I swung open the door of his business, passed the immobile weathervane and, without thinking about it, without making any decision, leapt onto the mountain he had forced me to see. When I was able to remove enough snow, I opened my car door and got in. It felt like a museum where you aren't allowed to touch anything. I leaned my forehead against the steering wheel out of pure instinct. And out of pure instinct I tried to see something through the windshield. To see something beyond the Snowy Place.

Simple Pleasure. Pure Pleasure.

She would remember everything, out of the blue and in full detail. She would see the jade ring wrapped around her ring finger and she would immediately see the other jade ring. She would open her eyes wide and, without knowing why, fall silent. She would say, Yes, very beautiful indeed. And she would run her fingertips over the delicate shape of the serpents.

A caress. The hint of a caress. An immobile hand underneath. An alabaster hand. A velvet island.

She crossed the city at dawn in the back of a taxi. She drifted between sleep and anxiety, her handbag pressed against her chest. The beginning of a long journey awaited her at the airport. She knew it, and knowing it produced a sense of unease. She couldn't tell when such a dislike for traveling had developed, that reluctance to set forth, then resigning herself, somewhat bitterly, to it. She frequently had nightmares before leaving, and, as she climbed the steps to the plane, she had premonitions of terrible things. The discovery of a chronic illness. A sudden death. Loneliness.

"This will be the last one," she quietly promised herself, then shook her head, unable to believe her own vow.

"Were you saying something?" the taxi driver asked, watching her in the rearview mirror.

"Nothing," she whispered. "Only that this will be my last trip."

The car slowed behind a long line of traffic. They both peered out the windows.

"An accident," he murmured.

But as they approached the site of the collision, they didn't see mangled cars or other signs of a crash. They rolled forward without knowing what was going on. They opened their eyes wide. They looked at the gray sky, the faces of the sleepy drivers, the shards of glass on the side of the road. It wasn't until they were about to leave the scene behind that they saw what had happened.

"But that's a body," he said, his voice sounding an alarm.

"A naked body," she said. "A body without a head."

She asked him to stop and wait for her. Once out of the car, she showed her identification to the police guarding the scene and crossed the yellow tape. She walked around the decapitated body and paused to look at the dead man's left hand. There, around his ring finger, at the edge of a large pool of blood, was the jade ring. Two entwined green serpents. An extremely delicate thing. The Detective shot her hand out toward the object but stopped short of touching it. There was something about the ring, something between the ring and the world, that blocked her contact. It was then that she looked at her own hand, immobile and large, suspended in the dawn air.

"It's getting late," she managed to hear. And he started the car.

There is a city within a head.

On her return, she asked about the decapitated man, but no one had any information. She searched the archived documents in the Bureau of Homicide Investigation and couldn't find anything. Even her assistant looked incredulous when she asked about the incident.

"Are you sure?" He looked at her sideways. "We would've heard about something like that."

"It isn't in the newspapers?" she asked. "It's not there, either?"

The young man shook his head and lowered his gaze. She couldn't stand his suspicion or his pity and rushed out of the office.

The taxi driver assured her that he remembered everything. He emptied his memory before her eyes, into her hands, in full detail. He remembered that the blocked-off body was in the second lane on the highway that ran to the airport. He remembered that it had no clothes and that the skin showed bruising. An abstract painting. Torture. He remembered the pool of blood and the strange angles that various parts of the body formed. He remembered there were already three or four police officers—here his memory was a little cloudy—around the body when she got out of the car to examine the scene. He remembered he had been the one to react: they had to get out of there if she wanted to catch her flight. She had to leave her position crouched next to the dead man if she wanted to get there in time. She did just that: she stood up. The sound of her knees. In the end, he remembered that, too: the sound of her knees. That.

"I've always wanted a ring like that," she said to the woman wearing it with detached elegance.

The woman lifted her hand, the back of it facing her eyes. It seemed as though she was looking at the ring for the first time.

"Do you really like it?"

"Yes," confirmed the Detective. "I'd still like to have one like it."

The woman turned to look at the illuminated waters of the pool, and, with melancholy or indifference, the Detective couldn't decide which, she raised a tall glass to her lips.

"It's from Asia," she said. "From the islands." She pronounced the words as if she weren't there, next to the pool, among the soothing murmurs of a crowd of people lolling away time at a party. "A gift," she concluded, placing the back of her hand before her eyes again. Her fingernails pointed toward the sky. "A gift from an excessively sentimental date."

"A lover's gift," the Detective quietly interjected. The woman smiled coolly.

"You could say that," she whispered. "Something like that."

She couldn't help it. Every time she met someone she asked herself the same questions. Is this person capable of killing? Am I standing before a victim or a murderer? Would this person resist at the crucial moment? Occupational hazards. When the woman turned around, moving away from the edge of the pool with the languor of another time—a slower though no less intense time—the Detective wasn't sure. She didn't know if the woman was capable of killing in cold blood, of cutting off a man's head and throwing his body onto the highway. She didn't know if the woman was the victim of a conspiracy made of jewels and narcotics and lies. She didn't know if her aloofness was a mask or a face already stripped of the mask. The woman intrigued her precisely because of this, because her attitude made it so that the Detective couldn't know anything about her.

"What is a ring, really?" she asked the Assistant without taking her hands off the steering wheel. "A manacle? A link in a chain? A symbol of belonging?"

"A ring can also be a promise," the young man interrupted. "Not every romantic gift has to be as terrible as you imagine."

The Detective turned to look at him. She twitched the right side of her mouth and asked him for a cigarette.

"But you don't smoke," he reminded her.

"I just want to hold it between my fingers," she said. "Go on."

"Are you sure it's the same ring? The same design?"

"The same design, yes. But it could be a coincidence. A tremendous coincidence. Anyway, we have other things to figure out. We don't have time to investigate murders no one reported. We don't get paid for that."

The two looked at one another out of the corners of their eyes and began to laugh. Then, below the red traffic light, they rolled down their windows and stared up at the sky.

"How do we start?"

There is a movie within a head.

She found her again, in the aisles of a grocery store. Goods. Prices. Tags. The Detective was looking for coffee filters while the Woman with the Jade Ring carefully analyzed, with a care that seemed more like scenography, several bottles of wine. The Detective watched her from afar as she decided how to approach: the woman's narrow shoulders, her long, straight hair, her high heels. She wasn't beautiful, but she was sophisticated. She was the kind of person who attracted people's attention.

"This is a tremendous coincidence," the Detective said by way of a greeting when she approached the woman with her hand outstretched.

"Do you come here often?" the woman responded, without any surprise, and leaned her face close to the Detective's to offer and receive the kisses of a more familiar greeting.

"Not really," she said as she smiled. "I only come here when I know I'll find the Woman with the Jade Ring in aisle eight, at three in the afternoon."

"Do you still want one like this?" She lifted her left hand again, her fingernails pointing toward the sky, to look at the ring.

"Would you sell it?"

The Woman with the Jade Ring let out a burst of shrill laughter, then took the Detective by the elbow and guided her toward the exit.

"Come," she said.

They climbed into the back of a black car that sped off. The Woman with the Jade Ring dialed a number on her cell phone and, turning toward the window, said something in a low voice and in a language the Detective didn't understand. They were soon traveling through narrow streets lined with stalls selling food and other goods. The smell of fried fat. The smell of incense. The smell of many bodies together. When the car finally arrived at its destination, the Detective had the sensation that she had traveled to another time zone, another country.

The woman hung up her phone. "I'm going to ask you for a favor," she warned. "I'm going to ask you to investigate something for me." It was impossible to know what was in her eyes behind the dark glasses she had donned when stepping into the sunlight, impossible to know what motivated the slight tremor in her lips. "Your job is to investigate things, right?"

As soon as the Detective nodded, she took her by the elbow again and led her through the crowd and under the awnings and through alleys. Finally, she opened a red wooden door, and, as if they at last found themselves safe after a long pursuit, they flopped down on overstuffed leather armchairs. A fragile man offered them water. Someone else turned on low music.

"The coincidence wasn't that tremendous, was it?" asked the Detective with her usual pride, trying to understand what was going on as quickly as she could.

"In any case, it isn't a very original request," the woman answered contemptuously.

"You want to tell me about the decapitated man that no one knows anything about. You want to tell me about the other ring." The Detective covered her mouth with the glass of water and, at the same time, looked around the room in which she found herself. The windows covered with thick velvet curtains. The floor made of soft wood. The spiderwebs in the corners. Perhaps that's where everything ends. Perhaps there was nothing else.

"Are you always so blunt?" the woman asked, her eyes half shut. The annoyance. The gestures of good manners.

"I suppose so. That," the Detective interrupted herself to take another sip of water, "is my job. That's how I make a living."

"I can pay you three times what you make."

"Make it four," she immediately responded. Then they started to talk.

Money always worked on her. Money and knowledge: two currencies. She was sure that at the end of it all, on receiving the agreed-upon amount, she would turn to laugh at herself in the mirror. Did she really need it? The water. The drops of water on her face. She would tell herself later what she told herself then: no, strictly speaking, I don't need it. She would add: the person who needs it, the person who needs to give it in return for what I will learn, is her. And then she would look again at the ring as she saw it the first time: a shackle, a trap, the last link in the chain that still tied the decapitated man to life. A sign. Discovery and money. The chain of the natural world. When she got under the sheets, she thought she wouldn't mind at all if they were made of silk.

She told the Detective the ring was a promise. A promise she had given and a promise she had received. A pact.

"A blood pact?" the Detective interrupted her, unable to conceal the taunt.

"Something like that," the woman answered, looking her straight in the eye. The woman told her she had also seen him on the highway. She had seen him, she clarified, without knowing it was him. Without even imagining it. She said her car had also slowed down and that, when she didn't see the accident, she had asked about the cause of the delay. She had to arrive on time. She said she held in her hands the ticket for a long journey, a journey to the East. And she showed it to the Detective at that moment. She showed her the ticket. An unused ticket. When he didn't arrive—she said this, too—when she confirmed that he hadn't arrived and that he would never again arrive, she turned around and went back home. She hadn't cried, she told the Detective.

She also told the Detective that she hadn't tried to figure anything out. That her curiosity came later. She told her that at first she was content to listen to the rumors that circulated among her drivers. She caught every other word from their hushed conversations: body, torture, head, hand. Then she heard the words that made reference to the site: the highway, the second lane, the airport. She said that, little by little, without really wanting it, she had pieced together the puzzle from echoes, whispers, secrets. All she was missing was the head, she told her. Because there is a city there. A movie. An entire life there. In the head.

The jade ring was a precious jewel. If it was really that same ring that appeared in the photographs the Detective had found on the designer's website, then she was before a highly valuable treasure. It came from Asia, indeed, but the designer belonged to two worlds: also an inhabitant of Main Metropolis for many years. The entwined serpents came from further back. From all of time. The motif that from afar seemed uniquely amorous was, on closer inspection, lethal. The serpents were opening their jaws. Face-to-face, in a state of stupor or alarm. The ring seemed to be of the exact size so that the teeth, though they were bared, didn't touch one another. It was a circle made to prevent injury. To exorcise it.

One serpent facing the other. Their mouths open. Their bodies entwined. A circular base under their bodies. The beginning of a movie. The beginning of a city. The Detective opened her eyes wide behind the windshield. The traffic's intermittent lights on the man, on the woman, that lay far away from everything, in another place. The roundness of their shoulders. Their parted lips. The smell of jasmine tea. One breathing into the other. The word: forever. The words: a velvet island. The words: here, within, everything is mine. One breathed out of the other.

She had gone to the Faraway City to continue the drug trafficking investigation. Days before, by a stroke of luck, the team had come across a name that was potentially important for the case. When they had to decide who would take the trip to follow up, the married and recently hired detectives pointed to her, as if the choice were obvious. At takeoff, still with the unease that traveling engendered in her and the vision of the decapitated head, she thought about the things that her single lifestyle forced her to do. Traveling the world, for example. Stopping for freshly dead bodies. Asking about the location of a head.

"Traveling for pleasure?" her seatmate had asked her, trying to strike up a conversation.

The Detective had shaken her head and closed her eyes. Pleasure. It had been a long time since she had done things for pleasure. Simple pleasure. Pure pleasure.

There is an airplane flying within a head.

"The order to stop our inquiry came from higher up," the Assistant whispered to her as they walked to the car. And he repeated it later, once they were seated at the table in the restaurant where they had chosen to eat.

"Lack of evidence," he continued. "You know. One more execution. One of many."

A chicken bone sticking out of his mouth. His fingers covered in grease.

His rapid words.

"And no one's found the head?"

"Never."

There is a body within a head. An alabaster hand. A ring.

She opened the door to her house. She took off her shoes. She put water on for tea. When she finally lay down on the couch, she realized she was not only exhausted but depressed. Something about the unattended homicide. One more execution. One of many. Something about having to embark on a journey to a faraway city. Something about life-sized statues destroyed by time. Broken limbs all around. Something about a woman who uses money to buy a head within which there is a city with many lights and a movie of two bodies together, a harmful breath, and an airplane taking off. Something about opening the door and taking off her shoes and making tea in a house in which a head floats within a head.

She went back to the scene of the crime. She told the taxi driver to wait for her while she poked around the weeds that bordered the highway. The thought arrived fully developed in her mind: I'm looking for a head. She raised her face toward the magnificent clarity of the sky. She breathed deeply. She didn't believe she was a woman looking for a head on the side of the highway to the airport. She looked back at the ground. Pebbles. Tracks. Litter. A scrap of fabric. A rusted can. Plastic. Cigarette butts. She touched some things. Most she looked at from afar. She was, indeed, a woman looking for a head on the side of the highway. She soon convinced herself that the crime hadn't taken place there. Here. She soon knew that this was just a scene that reflected what had happened somewhere else. Somewhere far away. Somewhere as far away as the East.

–

To lose your head. The man had done it. To lose everything you had within your head: a city, a movie, a life, a ring. What he had lost, she now gained: the connection between the lights of the city and the lights of the movie and the lights of the life and the lights of the ring. All of this luminosity on a circular base. The Detective suddenly saw it all again, blinded by the moment. Perhaps a dream: definitely a hallucination. There were the interwoven bodies again. The slowness with which the tip of the index finger glides over the skin of the belly, the embowed branches covering the pubis, the lips' edge. The subsequent spasm. There was the hand that decisively grabs the long, feminine hair. A bridle. The moans of pain. The moans of pleasure. Pure pleasure. Simple pleasure. The Detective wondered, many times, if it had been worth it. This: the shattering of the breath, the blank eyes, the crunch of the skeleton. The Detective had no way of knowing whether the man, if alive now, would have run the risk again.

There is pleasure—pure pleasure, simple pleasure—within a head.

The woman wasn't beautiful, but she was elegant. There was a veil between her and the world that made everything feel uneasy. Her way of walking. The way she lifted her hand to show, indifferently, teetering on a sense of boredom, that ring. A promise. She had said just that: a promise. A promise given. The Detective visited her to give her the bad news: no findings, no information. The man, whose name she hadn't dared utter, had disappeared without a trace. She couldn't do it any longer. She couldn't keep poring over old newspapers, through archives and documents. She couldn't keep prowling around the scene of a crime committed far away. She couldn't stand it anymore. She said it all like that, at once, in a rush. I can't keep investigating your case. No one could.

The Woman with the Jade Ring barely smiled. She offered her an iced tea. She invited her to sit in the springy armchair. Then she opened a door through which a tiny woman entered and knelt before the Detective and, without looking her in the eyes, skillfully and gently took off her shoes. Then she disappeared and came back with a little footstool upholstered with red velvet and a white basin filled with hot water from which arose aromas of herbs. With delicate movements, she helped the Detective place her bare feet in it. The most basic pleasure. Barely a moan. The spasm. The little woman then placed one of the Detective's feet on the stool, between her own parted legs. While she massaged the bottom of the Detective's foot, the tip of her thumb at the head of the metatarsals, the rest of her fingers on her instep, the Woman with the Jade Ring was silent. And that's how she remained as the masseuse's hands worked up the sides of the foot, as her thumb and index finger grabbed the Achilles tendon and massaged it in the same direction, firmly. Her open hand on her arch, then. And, later, at a time she no longer recognized, while the woman clutched her knee with her left hand, softly bending it, the Detective felt an immense desire to scream. The pain forced her eyes open. She opened her lips. She exhaled. There, before her, suspended in the air in the Woman with the Jade Ring's hand, outstretched just at that moment, was the promised money.

"Good work," she congratulated her.

The Detective bowed her head but lifted her gaze. Her elbows on her knees. The money in her hand and her feet in the tepid, aromatic water. A strange image. An out-of-place image. The corruption of the senses.

I always wanted a ring like that. I want one still.

Strange Is the Bird that Can
Cross the River Pripyat

⊗

[Electronica music]

This is what the Young Woman listens to through her headphones while she jumps (her hair tied up) (her hands in a fist) (her feet far from the ground) with her eyes closed:

Intro-percussions-(eq+bass)-piano chords **Kontakt** (delay)-piano melody **Kontakt** (**filter** band pass)-synthesized chords from the Vst A1 **Waldorf**, Warm Pad sound (**filter** low-pass 24 Db), Velocity 50%, modulation+3, oscl+2 in sync, chorus/flanger 90% depth 100%, mixer 70%, ring Mod 65& Osc2 50%, PW Mod 90%, PW 50%, _Detune 45%, Square, **LFO** Speed 50%, Range 3, Glide on 25% **ADSR OSC1** normal, **ADSR** OSC2 normal (50%,45%,50%,75%)—ambient Harmony Vst A1 Thin Whistles WFM (**filter** high-pass 12 DB, cutoff 54%, Velocity 60%, modulation+6, oscl+2 in sync, chorus/flanger 50% depth 100%, mixer 50%, ring Mod 35% Osc2 50%, PW Mod 60%, PW 40%, _Detune 0%, Square, **LFO** Speed 50%, Range 3, Glide off 0% **ADSR OSC1** (30%,60%,75%,80%), **ADSR OSC2** (50%,60%,30%,40%). Bass drum 4x4 (sample drum, sharp EQ, compressor 45%) Congas Kontakt (sample drum, medium EQ, spectral delay 5%). Bass VST VB-1 Warm Bass (shape 40%, detune 66%, Vol-1.93, pickups), Rhythm with Vocoder drum sample, filtered electribe and electroharmonics of various types.

The open window in front of her. The breeze through the curtains. A sudden change in the shades of gray. All of it stops her cold. All of it (that she does not perceive) (or that she perceives but does not know she perceives) makes her walk in a straight line, warily, across the square tiles. The headphones over her ears. Soles on marble.

This is what she sees when she pulls back the curtains: an abandoned city. There are tall rectangular buildings. There are parks covered in snow. There are white rooftop terraces. Groves. A frozen river. Black birds. Giant iron ships. An in-the-distance. A there-is-nothing-more. The gray sky, impenetrable, over all of it. Over Pripyat.

When she looks out the window and feels the prickling of the air on her face, the only thing that surprises her is the silence. Heavy. Omnipresent. Scandalous. She had never heard it before. That's what it seems like: that never. Before.

This is what she does (in strict chronological order): she blinks while something inside her tries to explain / transcribe / translate what her eyes see; she stifles a wail of impotence or of frustration or of nothing; she turns around; she pulls the headphones from her ears; she runs to the door she opens the door she walks through the door; she sprints down the stairs (the palm of her right hand on the iron handrail); she crosses the building's landing (the palm of her left hand on her stomach); she opens the front door, crosses the street, and, once outside, stops in the very center of the small plaza, solitary as a flagpole; quivering, imprisoned by the onset of nausea, she realizes she is cold.

The silence, first; the cold, after. She between the two extremes.

On the way back (while she trembles) (while she grips her forearms) (while she thinks about how strange the expression "goose bumps" is), she feels it once again. The unimaginable is still there. That which you cannot conceive.

Her mind blank. That curtain. That layer of ice.

In the room, upon closing the window while still looking down (a herd of horses on the asphalt), she has no alternative. She has to accept it. This is all that happens: there is a girl alone in an empty city.

All this beneath the sound of the electronica music that (still) plays through the headphones.

⊗

[The man and the boy]
She sees them for the first time (although she doesn't realize it)

183

on her way back to her apartment. She goes quickly but still sees them (although without seeing them) through a partly open door. Her rapid breathing and the violent beating of her heart keep her from noticing anything, but she sees them around a rectangular table, faintly illuminated by an alcohol or gas lamp. It's an Elderly Man with thin white hair. And it's a Skinny Boy. Two skeletons. Two statues. No noise between the two.

The second occasion in which she sees them (though for her it's the first) takes place when, minutes after thinking the phrase "there is a girl alone in an empty city," she decides to turn off the walkman and take off the headphones. There below, on the empty streets, the galloping of a herd of horses. The sound of hooves on asphalt. The whinnying. There below, in one of the rooms of her building, something. She goes slowly this time (pensively).

"I thought I was the only one," she murmurs as she carefully pushes the door open. The grinding of time. The aperture of color.

The Man and the Boy lift their faces in unison. The little one smiles at her (a gesture executed on its own) while the Elderly Man looks at her transfixed, without blinking, without an expression on his face. The letters: PRIPYAT: carved into the wooden table. Fractures. A coded message.

"We did too," the Boy says quietly. "We didn't think anyone else was left."

The breeze through the curtains. The pungent smell of something (still) unknown. The silence of the color gray.

"What is your jacket made of?" the Elderly Man then asks her. Still without blinking; still without an expression on his face.

She (without really noticing) (automatically) lowers her gaze, but, before reaching any conclusion about the material her jacket is made of, when she is about to figure out what she is doing, she lifts her eyes and confronts him. The Boy, then, takes her by the elbow and slowly guides her (as if she or he were sick) to the other side of the door. Outside.

The putrid smell. The hexagonal skylight and a sunbeam. The expanse of the internal space. The sound on the fragile wooden steps.

"He's worried about the future," the Boy whispers. Then he smiles at her as if that explains everything.

⊗

[Exterior context]
Here, on this white paper, on what is still called a page, there is a snowflake just before it turns into water.

This is the wetness that is coming.

The thing undone.

A tree grows inside a house.

⊗

[Interior context]
Within this page there is a Very Young Woman who silently repeats the phrase "strange is the bird that can cross the River Pripyat." As she does it, as the silence repeats this phrase within her head and three ships run aground in a bend of the navigable tributary of the Dnieper and the radioactive cloud becomes a

soft violet color around her head, the Girl does nothing but think about the possibility of crossing the Pripyat River. The possibility of not being a bird.

⊗

[Head like a crystal ball]

The Elderly Man gets up from his seat, buttons his jacket and (slowly) (with difficulty) takes the three steps that separate him from the window as if they were long empty kilometers. A mountain range. A plain in flames. The desert battered by the winds of the Harmattan.

He says: Turkana (without turning around to see the undaunted faces of the Boy and the Girl).

He says: There is a place called Magadi (still without looking at them).

And the voice that travels from the numbing crystal of the window to the Boy's red ears and the Young Woman's carries something celestial and something of another unknown (nonexistent) color. That kind of longing. That kind of form that longing sometimes takes.

He says: I don't know if we'll make it (and then he turns his head and, almost at the same time, his torso; finally, his feet).

The Boy and the Young Woman (motionless) don't know what to do before the (hollow) (dazed) (difficult to describe) gaze of the Man who now gives the impression of being younger. Above his head the soft swaying of a crystal chandelier. Encircling everything: the cracks (horizontal) that crisscross the walls, turning them into maps of places about to disappear. Behind him: beyond the window: the solid white of the Dnieper. On the man's (skinny) body: a black jacket.

"He's dreaming," murmurs the Boy when, standing on tip-toes, he is able to reach the Girl's ear. "He's dreaming about the island."

Then this happens: the Elderly Man takes the three steps that separate him from the narrow wooden table (nimbly) (as if he were in a virtual world): his arms extended: his gaze effectively stunned: and he places each of his open hands (long fingers) (prominent knuckles) on either side of the child's skull.

He closes his eyes. He is silent. He opens his eyes.

(Between one thing and the next, entire years pass: between one thing and the next the world ends: a world begins.)

Then they appear. Then they take a clear shape. The first image is of an accumulation of (square) adobe houses where a great (as-tonishing) quiet reigns. The second image, almost juxtaposed, is of a vast (never-ending) (flat) field dotted with sprigs, plants, herbs: all of that yellow color that came from the fire. The third image is full of crosses (sizes) (colors). There is another in which a ship has run aground in the middle of the (salty) (pure poison) sea. And one more in which (angular) dirt alleyways open onto small adobe cupolas: adobe igloos: small chambers of spaceships: promontories of soft lines in the earth.

The Boy and the Young Woman (motionless) (numb from the

cold) don't see the images (they cannot) (there are no images) but they listen with growing joy, with something like dread, in disbelief, with all their attention, to the (detailed) (longed for) descriptions that the Suddenly Rejuvenated Man gives without closing his eyes (suddenly blind) and without moving his hands that encircle the smallest one's skull.

From the other side of the window: the remains of a nuclear power plant.

He says: the journey will be long.

Then he sits down at the table again and places his right hand beneath his pointed chin as a support, and the left, like a mast, on his forehead that, little by little, fills with brown splotches, soft wrinkles. Again.

"I was wrong" the boy murmurs, standing on tiptoes again to reach the Young Woman's crimson ear. "He isn't dreaming about the island. This time he isn't dreaming about the island."

"What then?" asks the Young Woman who has to crouch down to reach the boy's ear.

"He's dreaming about Asyut," the (current) (final) tone of a statement of fact.

"We are now a tribe," the Elderly Man murmurs to himself, hiding his gaze, covering his eyes. "We're a clan."

⊗

[Why do you set forth on a journey to a cemetery?]

Because you are alone. Because a bird has crashed into the windowpane and because the winter gusts shatter the porcelain mugs. Because there is nothing else to do. Because there is a girl alone in the middle of an empty plaza. Because the past no longer exists. Because, suddenly, a city has crumbled away. Because she is curious. Because the color of the screen is still white. Because strange is the bird that can cross the River Pripyat. Because the bony hand of a boy almost produces heat. Because the jacket is made of a resistant material. Because the headphones no longer work. Because the walls are cracked. Because she wants to talk. Because the gray sky is immense, immeasurable, infinite. Because a man sees the images of his longing in the head of a boy. Because the shoes that sink into the snow leave footprints like miniscule lakes. Because the electronica music continues playing in the woman's ears. Because she doesn't yield and she has yet to ask why. Because there is no one else. Because this is the day after the night after hearing the quiet for the first time. Because the dead bird lies on the bench of a world that has ceased to be. Because we are within the head of a woman who sees photographs of brutal beauty. Because there are tin cans that rattle, cracking a strange music, with the passing gusts of wind. Because there once was a world full of trains. Because you are hungry. Because you are thirsty. Because the echo of a longing voice produces longing. Because there are black cables tangled around the table legs. Because the electric light makes a disturbing noise. Because there is a girl alone who spins in the middle of an empty plaza as she screams the names of people who do not exist. Because of the echo. Because of that echo. Because the horses they brought from the steppe gallop, crazed. Because the tattered flags flutter in the waves of the air. Because a solitary girl steps on the body of a bird that, after charging into the windowpane, lies dead on a bench in a world that still is. Because strange is the bird. Because the girl sobs. Because the speakers look like the unyielding eyes of the departed. Because the tears are sharp. Because they wound. Just because. Because why not?

⊗

[Now, in this moment, the Boy and the Elderly Man and the Young Woman set forth on their journey to Asyut]
    The noise of their steps. Chlap. Chlop. Chlac.
    The noise of fear within their veins. Pum. Pam. Pum.
    The noise shrk crgg kgh of thoughts racing.

⊗

[Landscape as premonition]
Before reaching the river, before trying to cross in a phantom ferry, the Boy and the Elderly Man and the Young Woman have to see these images:
    The black of a bird (or something) that crosses, like a rippling stain, the grayish mantle of the sky. A sort of flickering. A glow (the opposite of).
    The buildings, rectangular. The streets. The streetlamps leaning over the asphalt. The cables.
    The trucks, arrested. The helicopters, on the side of the path. The tractors. The bicycles (without handlebars). A stroller. The military tanks. The tires. The color of rust over all of it.

They have to see the tall, equidistant electric towers. The cables. The blades of the giant fans. The Ferris wheel (yellow seats, blue umbrellas).

The leafless trees. The numb brush. The thin and frozen branches (getting thinner and thinner) (freezing more and more). The land. The earth beneath the weight of the snow and boots: a map of holes.

They have to see the lit forest. A rotten, red forest. That stain in the distance.

And the rain: the way the drops appear and disappear from the field of vision (fugitive lines). The rain like a pure, uninterrupted drop. That sensation. That flash. The way the (tiny) drops are pelting down on their cheeks: a crash more than a caress. The sound (that can be seen) of the drops: waves. The dirty sound of the electric recorder. Waves. A breakdown. As if it were living, an organism that breathes in and out. Waves. Is this, then, the body of the rain? An absent biology. A thing already gone.

The mutism (the quiet) (the lethargy) of the nature that, all together, all at the same time, lets the danger be felt, inviting it.

⊗

[A human noise]
The Elderly Man runs and, behind him, holding hands, the Young Woman and the Boy leave thin shadows in the mud (labored breathing). The sounds of the brushing of the jackets against the branches of the pines. The Boy (without warning) (without transition) screams, an unknown scream, a scream in a foreign

191

language, a scream that is a pure scream, the Elderly Man stops (static eyes) (internal organs in expansion). Alabaster statues (or marble). Sudden ice. A gesture.

The breathing, the inhale and the exhale, is all that can be heard in the middle of the darkness. The breathing.

All this happens in a place that cannot be seen. Inside.

Barely a minute later a shot is heard and, immediately, the echo of the shot (sound that fades) (sound in fugue). The hush continues (ominous) (frightening). Then the Boy mutters the word *Asyut*.

      And everything comes to a stop. Stock-still. A natural catalepsy.

"Let's go," the Elderly Man stammers, much later, with intertwined firmness and sweetness. A tremor. It is an order, of this there is no doubt; an order provoked by fear (uneasiness). A "let's go" that is not really pointing in any direction.

"Then there's someone else," the Young Woman devises without being able to move. Marble statue (or alabaster). And her voice suddenly acquires the same consistency as the ice that shatters (fragile) under her (non-existent) steps.

"Let's go," the Elderly Man repeats, much later, but no one takes the first step.

⊗

[What the Elderly Man says while he encircles the boy's head with both hands]

He talks about Asyut as if he were in a trance (he is in a trance). He says: it is a city of the dead. A real city of the dead! Everyone there is dead. Those who rest are dead and those who don't rest are dead. The houses are houses for the dead. Those who live there (which is merely a figure of speech) are dead. Dead are those who walk through the streets and dead are those who look out the open doors with their sunken dead eyes. Dead is the sky above Asyut and, beneath its ground, dead is the dead earth. Barren from before. Barren from forever more. Dead is the bird that flies above the disaster and dead is the insect of unnerving colors that crawls and collapses and digs until it finds or constructs the niche of its own death, the eternal. The solitary dead. Dead are the white teeth of the dead and the cavity-filled molars of the dead and the fingernails of the dead that claw at the skin of the other dead. There are corpses and pieces of corpses on the street. Asyut. We are all going to Asyut.

And his face is rejuvenated.

[What we no longer are]
They board the ferry as if it were an ark. A final opportunity. Behind: the city and the forest and the Invisible Sniper. Behind: the keyboard and the television and the photographs. Behind: the wind that, when it shakes a curtain or a blade or an object that is otherwise stationary, unsettles or startles. A bathtub. A monumental empty pool. The avenues. Behind the herds of horses that gallop through a city without men or women or

children. They are left with the now; the here. They are now crossing the navigable sections of the river. The Young Woman directs to the Elderly Man (a question) (a last-minute thought) and the Elderly Man shrugs his shoulders (indifference) (don't bother me) as his only response. Then he turns his gaze toward the sky (ah, the infinite) (what no longer exists). The Boy's eyes oscillate between the Man who turns his head up and the frustrated grimace of the Young Woman. It is then that he places his fingers (bony) (almost transparent) on the back of the feminine hand and, in the contact, almost generates heat. Something tepid: a bird's breath.

"Look," says the Elderly Man pointing with his index finger beneath the surface of the water. "We are no longer that."

What they see is the following: screens, shoes, tires, antennas, diapers, fabric, headphones, photographs, pills, doors, glass, books, boxes, glasses, cadavers.

"No longer," he insists.

And the Young Woman with the face of a screen, shoe, tire, antenna, diaper, fabric, headphone, photograph, pill, door, glass, book, box, glasses, cadaver, looks at him (she cannot believe him) (she cannot help but feel a sudden fear) with shock.

The three flow like the water beneath the thin layer of ice that covers the flowing Pripyat.

⊗

[The guest]
They had seen the ferry as if it were a dream or a ghost (The Flying Dutchman), she remembers that now, sitting with her arms

wrapped around her knees (the woman like a cradle for herself), trying to generate a little body heat. They had jumped joyously, jubilantly, and later, pressured by the Elderly Man, had covered their mouths with their hands, that is what she sees upon closing her eyes (woman who touches four damp walls). When they finally leapt toward the moving structure (the pain in their knees) (the fear of slipping) she heard, of this she is sure, as she hears now, and of this she is also sure, that voice that repeats again and again: "strange is the bird that can cross the River Pripyat." She knows that if she smiles the cold will hurt her gums and teeth (burning on her lips). She knows the ferry advances because she hears the noise (something that breaks) that the keel makes upon colliding with the thin layer of ice that covers the Pripyat waters. But the voice. A bird that flies. Strange, yes. Nothing in the sky.

"Look," stammers the boy in her ear (the smell of rotting teeth), suddenly surprised. Then, upon noting the lack of reaction from the Girl, he lifts his index finger toward the engine room. "Do you see it?"

The premonition. The fear. The desire to run away.

"It's a man," he says, hesitating. "Or something," he retracts.

The Young Woman tenses her neck (state of alarm), lifts her chin (curiosity): she wants to see. She wouldn't know what to do in that situation. The possibility of seeing another, anyone. But she quickly stands up, takes the Boy by the hand and walks forward, cautiously (the beating of her heart), hopefully (the pulse in her wrists), among other people's debris (spoons, suitcases, shoes) and the rust of the floor, over there.

"Are you sure?" In her eyes a hole through which the air flows.

"No," he answers, ashamed. "Not really. It seemed."

A Boy and a Young Woman stopped in their tracks (alabaster figures) in the doorway of a room where only the sound of the engine is heard. The purring. The keel whirls. Nothing in the sky.

"What are we going to find in Asyut?" the boy asks (the sweetness in his voice) without letting go of her right hand.

"The color of the sky there is blue," she murmurs as her only response, looking at him. Then, loosening the pressure on his hand, the Young Woman pulls something out of the right pocket of her jacket. She kneels down. Eye to eye; head to head. Clumsy (gloved hand), she manages to open the small package (the image of an onion) so that a hardboiled egg appears (*appears* is the correct word) before their eyes.

The smile then. Radiant, the corner of his lips. Infinite, the happiness of children. Of crazy people. Of imbeciles.

When they turn their heads at the same time, as if both responding to an animal instinct or a military order, they are confronted with the gaze of the moose that, attracted by the smell of the egg, has left his warm spot (unthinkable) behind the machines. Numbers. Red levers. Circles.

"Let's go to Asyut," she murmurs again, now close to his ear. "In Asyut the sky is blue," she repeats. "You'll see."

⊗

[One always hopes]

A bird is a message. A form of writing on the page of the sky. An excuse to lift your eyes and get lost in dark, oscillating thoughts. Another way of moving across the horizon. Black ink. Red ink. White ink. The melancholy that subtly overcomes. The pain that provokes the closeness of the distant, another way of saying this is impossible. A caricature. A metaphor. That which is in place of. A pair of post-historic wings. The beak that rips apart. The roundness of the unblinking eye. Dirty, the feathers. Footsteps on sand or in memory.

"Why didn't you leave earlier?" the Young Woman asks the Elderly Man when the Boy (finally) falls asleep on her lap. A moose at his feet. The purring of the machines.

Instead of answering, the Man examines the sky through the fogged glass of the window.

"Here," he offers. The Woman hesitates but then opens her hand to receive a handful of many small things. Trifles.

"Bread?" The shock in her voice, the trembling in her voice, the emotion.

"Look," he interrupts her. "Look there."

Infinite is the happiness of children and crazy people and imbeciles.

"Is that really a bird?" she manages to ask later, much later, incredulous. Clumps of bread between her teeth. Rye. The gaze after the sky: outward.

"A bird is a message," the man stammers. "Black ink on the sky," he murmurs and winks at the same time. "Look how close everything is." His hands are in the air, his gaze on the horizon. "Even what's in the distance."

Radiant, the smile on his face. Luminous, the eternity. A whirlwind made of hands and saliva and hair.

"Even what's gone," he concludes, looking at her.

The silence that emerges. That fills. Arouses. How much time afloat on a river? What does it mean to flow?

"I hoped everything would fade away," she whispers in the ear of the boy sleeping on her lap as she rocks and rocks him, embracing him, protecting him from the cold and from the Man who wraps his hands around his head. "One always hopes. I hoped everything would be left behind. Erased and crossed out, forever. I hoped. But nothing, not even the bird, faded away."

The exhaustion of her voice. The hunger. The thirst. Her eyes closed.

"One always hopes," the Elderly Man whispers. "Yes."

"Don't you dare," she warns him, stopping the hands that approach, desirously, the infantile skull. "Let him rest."

Too much time afloat on a river. The boredom. The passing of seconds, minutes, hours, days.

"You need to see this as much as I do," he vehemently states. "If we don't see it, we're going to die," he says without any tremor in his voice. "Is that what you want? Is that why you waited so long to escape?"

The Young Woman looks at him in awe. She doesn't know how to answer. She does not know what to do when the man kneels down in front of the Boy's head and, murmuring incomprehensible words, imprisoned by the glow emanating from the Boy's eyes, places the palms of his hands around the skull.

⊗

[Short films]

"Look," he invites her. "Watch this. There are lines of women in front of green trucks. Do you see the scars on their foreheads? They shiver from the cold. They pray. They make necklaces with their teeth. We are no longer all of that," he finally exclaims. "We," he stops short.

"Look," he insists. "The men go from one side to the other, without a path. They rub their hands together. They cry. They spit out teeth and viscera. Ice. They yearn. There's a cow there," he stops short, pensively.

"Look," he softens his voice. "There's a piano in the room. Imagine the music, go on. A tree grows inside. The loops of paint, look how they fall. A curtain that moves. The photographs."

"Look," he utters, excited. "The gesture," he signals something in the middle of the air and, when he realizes the woman cannot see it, that the woman cannot see anything, he gets discouraged. "The gesture of someone," he concludes, in a low voice.

"Look," he exclaims. "Now it's us! You, the Boy, and me, we are walking through the city and then on the snow, among the red plants. We're going over the river, look. I'm leaning against the two of you, I embrace you and then my right hand touches your breast under your jacket. The beating of your heart. Your skin."

⊗

[This beating]

The Young Woman remembers it upon running aground, she remembers everything. This:

> **Intro-percussions**-(eq+bass)-piano chords **Kontakt** (delay)—piano melody **Kontakt** (**filter** band pass)-synthesized chords from the Vst A1 **Waldorf**, Warm Pad sound (**filter** low-pass 24 Db), Velocity 50%, modulation+3, oscl+2 in sync, chorus/flanger 90% depth 100%, mixer 70%, ring Mod 65& Osc2 50%, PW Mod 90%, PW 50%, _Detune 45%, Square, **LFO** Speed 50%, Range 3, Glide on 25% **ADSR OSC1** normal, **ADSR** OSC2 normal (50%,45%,50%,75%)—ambient Harmony Vst A1 Thin Whistles WFM (**filter** high-pass 12 DB, cutoff 54%, Velocity 60%, modulation+6, oscl+2 in sync, chorus/flanger 50% depth 100%, mixer 50%, ring Mod 35% Osc2 50%, PW Mod 60%, PW 40%, _Detune 0%, Square, **LFO** Speed 50%, Range 3, Glide off 0% **ADSR OSC1**(30%,60%,75%,80%), **ADSR OSC2** (50%,60%,30%,40%). Bass drum 4x4 (sample drum, sharp EQ, compressor 45%) Congas Kontakt (sample drum, medium EQ, spectral delay 5%). Bass VST VB-1 Warm Bass (shape 40%, detune 66%, Vol-1.93, pickups), Rhythm with Vocoder drum sample, filtered electribe and electroharmonics of various types.

As the music inundates her left ear, she remembers the rest of it. The beating of her heart. The fear before the silence. The surprise of his appearance. The verdict: I will leave. The marble tiles. The passing of days and weeks and months and years. Decades. The verdict: I will wait longer. I am something (a bird, perhaps) that can cross the River Pripyat. The city envelops me, empty. The verb *to gallop*. An embrace. Is this a Man and a Boy? I am a seeing machine. The flow of blood beneath the skin. This beating.

The foot on the mud, sinking. The breath: something that is agitated inside. She is about to say: *we are lost as soon as we set foot on the ground*, but, before saying it, before the phrase slips from her tongue and crosses, whole, through the striated passageway of her mouth, she laughs. Laughter like the gallop of horses brought from the steppe. Laughter like a black message that crosses the sky with its beak on its back. Laughter like an invitation to bend over, shaking.

"Let's go," insists the Man, extending his hand to her. "There's no time to lose."

"We are a clan," the Boy whispers. All the fear in his voice. "Let's go."

When the Young Woman falls to her knees on the quagmire; when, pensive or exhausted, she hides her face in her own chest, exclaiming words, or pieces of words, that struggle to exist outside, in the open, the Elderly Man approaches her. A trembling hand on her hair. The gaze of the moose. The gaze of the Boy. The gaze of the bird that flies overhead. This beating.

"We've done it," he tells her in a quiet voice. "We've crossed the Pripyat," he insists, placing his hand over the jacket, over the Woman's chest. Forehead to forehead. The nose. The mouth. The closeness of the mouths, the faces.

The Woman then lifts her head and looks at him, the Man, as if across time. As if across a catastrophe.

"Asyut doesn't exist," she murmurs again and again. "Asyut," she says. An exhalation.

The Man, desperate in his task around the body of the woman and of the boy and the animal, spitting saliva and blasphemies, again places the palms of his hands around the child's skull.

"But Ilinstí does," he proclaims, haughtily. "Look," he insists. "Shepelichi exists."

Infinite is the joy of crazy people and imbeciles. Radiant, the smile. Atrocious are the images that the voice describes from the future.

One of these towns is Ilintsí, where some twenty people now live, among whom can be found Anna Oníkonevna Kalitá, eighty-two years old, known simply as Grandma Anna. She lives in a humble wooden house with her husband, Grandpa Mijaíl, two cows, some pigs, domestic fowl, and their faithful dog, a skinny little skittish mutt.

Among the hundreds of people who live in the area, two are famous: Grandpa Savka, seventy-six years old, and his wife, who are the only inhabitants of the town of Shepelichi, just three kilometers from the power plant. They were in the news last year, when the President visited them. Soon after, they were given a couple of piglets as a gift from the Chief of State.

⊗

[What the bird sees]
An impossible world there below.
A man and a woman and a boy and a moose: stains on the land-scape.

The shadow of its own flight on the page.

PART IV

DIMINUTUS

Reincarnation

She had seen herself at his side as they walked by the foyer mirrors: they were a sad couple.

Foyer mirrors are frequently beveled.

The affliction was and was not in their garments: a sky-blue sheath on her body and a light gray suit on his.

The affliction could be heard in the ringing of her heels on the marble floor.

The affliction is a matter of an excess of order.

Is the affliction the same as heartbreak?

Surely she had wondered that before.

I do not know what he might have wondered.

If instead of going to a party they had stayed home alone, without a doubt they would have cried.

Without a doubt: that phrase frightens me.

There is the possibility that the man and woman would have remained silent in their separate rooms in the same house.

Large houses adjust themselves to the solitude of their inhabitants.

A complete sentence is like a room where a woman and a man cry without so much as noticing it.

Sadness is frequently expressed through sobs.

It is also common for sadness to turn out to be inexpressible.

Is sadness the same as the affliction?

The man could not believe she would repeat the words of a fortune teller.

The woman had already explained to him the difference between a riddle and a reincarnation.

Something will be said.

The man would have preferred that she were a sleepwalker.

If she had been a sleepwalker, he could have saved her from the precipice.

Sleepwalking women tend to wear long white dresses.

You talk in your sleep, she had assured him somewhat bellicosely.

To afflict is a verb that comes from the Latin *affligere*.

To afflict refers to both physical suffering and moral torment.

A demand: I want my perceptions to change me.

Those who hold power spend a large part of their time ensuring that the man and woman are suitably reproduced.

Nearby, someone was playing an old music box.

The man could not believe that the woman insisted that reincarnation is a way of coming back.

The man could not believe that his sadness, his affliction, that physical suffering and moral torment could be transmitted through the words he uttered while asleep.

No one has any idea who the first afflicted man on Earth was. That is true.

Dumbfounded can be an adjective or a noun.

While they were chatting around a small table in the back garden, a windowpane split in two.

The crashing of glass when it breaks.

We had a son. He died when he was two years old.

The spectator comes to watch how the actor wears out.

A couple hurries past the beveled mirrors of a foyer.

If I had to guess, I would say that this all happens in 1947.

A show is a duration.

There is someone who is quiet and someone who talks while a peculiar music floats through the broken window that looks out on a back garden.

A woman holds a boy in her arms, against her chest, in an airplane.

Aside from airport security, air travel is a fast mode of transportation.

In 1947, airport security was not as rigorous.

The man could not believe that the woman had carried a dead boy in her arms.

The affliction is a toll on the body.

What has been said becomes materially unerasable.

Language is like this.

She would have insisted that a prediction is different from a re-incarnation.

People do not usually cry in their homes but in a graveyard.

Some cemeteries have become tourist attractions.

The actor is a dead man who speaks, a corpse that looks like me.

Death is frequently an error and it is also inevitable.

Unforgiveable occurrences stop the passage of time.

The crime is a place to which you have to return.

Language is like that.

The same can be said about an accidental death.

She would have sworn the death of the infant wasn't her fault.

If she had been a sleepwalker, he would have been able to push her off the precipice.

To become a murderer or a murderess is a relatively easy task.

You talk in your sleep, she had insisted with the same rage.

I prefer the word *ire* to the word *rage*.

At one point, the man would have been able to see the boy's body in the woman's arms.

Sometimes it is necessary to drink a fine cognac.

I hope you stop considering your bodies as intelligent telegraphs.

Given it is full of orifices, many things pass through the body.

Tears are not a sign of something else.

The affliction is very similar to heartbreak, in any case.

The couple that walks by the foyer's beveled mirrors is in a hurry to turn around.

Did a world without remorse ever exist?

Painstakingly tended gardens give the appearance of being closed off.

There is a woman in the process of opening her arms.

Let someone utter the words: I brought him back to you.

The embrace tends to be taken as a sign of welcome or of peace.

The Infusion

The noise distracted me. It was something small, a gentle scratching. Or stubborn rattle in the cupboard. I left the notebook in which I was jotting some additions or subtractions on the formica table and blindly followed the thread of sound. I leaned out the windows just to check that the village was still dark and quiet. I opened the front door, but no one was there with a question or to be let in. A little nervous, I put water on to boil in a pewter basin thinking I would make a cup of tea. Again, I sat at the table. When I calmed down, back at work with my calculations, the noise started again. This time I knew instinctively where it was coming from. It was the pantry, without a doubt. Two strides. The anticipation. Turning the doorknob, I pictured a giant rat.

"And who are you?" I asked the woman crouching in the corner of the dark room where I stored a few canned goods and the mops. The woman, surprised, only managed to lift her head. Her mouth open. Pieces of nuts between her lips. I assumed that was her way of telling me she wasn't sure where she was, or who, or even what she was going to be. What are you really looking at when you stare at someone for that long?

"But it's cold in here," I said, pulling her by the arm. She resisted at first, but as soon as she realized I wouldn't hurt her, she let herself be led to the kitchen. The water was already boiling. Turning my back to her, I prepared the infusion. The water fell over the strainer where some herbs were whirling. The aroma. My eyes, closing.

I started talking to her without really knowing why. I suppose everyone who comes close is at first just an annoying noise inside a room. With my back to her, I made some comment about the hard times we were facing, how the potato harvest had been destroyed by a fungus and the water well had suddenly dried up. "Didn't you notice how desolate everything is?" I asked turning around to face her. "All you need to do is check the roof of the church, half devastated by earthquakes and summer cloudbursts. You didn't notice it, did you?" The woman looked at me, quizzically. Her arms by her sides. "It's useless, isn't it," I said, as I went back to the business of pouring the boiling water. The steam swirling gently from the mug of tea.

"Look," I said as I turned once again. That was the first time I saw her smile. I pulled out one of the chairs and invited her to sit down. I offered her some bread, a little butter, some salt. I explained I didn't have much more. That I had gotten sidetracked. That once again I'd forgotten to go to the co-op for the groceries I'd been rationed. I opened the pantry door where I'd found her and said, to confirm what she already knew: it's empty. My puttering about the room made her laugh. She covered her mouth with her right hand and then somewhat shyly adjusted the scarf that kept her long smooth hair in its place.

"Do you want to shower?" I asked. Her face was stained with something that could have been dirt, or time. Her clothes smelled of roads and caves and sweat and roots buried deep in the ground. But I was offering her the bathroom for something else. She looked tired and lost. Famished. I thought a warm shower could do her good. She stared at me without blinking, trying hard to understand what I was saying. I made signs: my hands on my head, like water; my hands on my torso, as if with soap; my hands around my forearms, as a towel's embrace. When nothing worked, I invited her to stand up from her chair and then led her to the bathroom. I turned on the tap. I said: See?

Yes, she saw. She saw everything. With a couple of gesticulations, she asked me to leave, and I returned to the kitchen to wait for her with the herb infusion.

The shapes of steam are sometimes bodies.

I imagined what would happen next. She was going to leave and come back, many times. That was—and I guessed it from the very moment her mouth noises interrupted the additions and subtractions with which I was trying to calculate the proper distribution of grain in the village, in the event of drought—her only way of staying. She appeared out of nowhere and into nowhere she would go with a regularity that I would come to call astonishing. She would learn my language and I hers with the passing of the days. With the passing of the days, in fact, we would create words and peculiar forms to describe objects, scenes, emotions, temperaments. Our own alphabet. An untransferable and unique grammar. When a bird would pause, watching our interaction through the windows, that bird would confirm its suspicions:

215

people are bizarre. But how strange they are, it would repeat in its own way, those creatures with two legs and a head, those creatures with mouths and hands! When our neighbors would by chance overhear our quiet conversations, those conversations that made us laugh uncontrollably, madly, they would shake their heads, fearing the worst. We would talk like that for a long time, around the table that had become a valley, in the warm, infinite, terrible rectangle of the bed, under the humble lintels of the doors. I would learn, at her side, a strange form of happiness. She would tell me something about the place she came from, her friends, her family. She would describe the flora and fauna. She would use the word "wild" many times. We would create cities and names of cities and maps so that the names could be matched to the cities. We would divide the time into the yesteryear and the nowadays and in that divided time we learned to fall silent, spying on each other, our fingertips, our breath.

And then, one afternoon, one winter afternoon, to be more exact, we noticed it. This, the farewell. This the slow, sad, unique way of coming unstuck from the language and the objects and the hands.

And I would remember that night then, that other winter night when the noise from her mouth had distracted me from planning for the drought, forcing me to take the necessary strides to open the door of a deserted pantry. And again I would open it, that door, this empty pantry, even convincing myself I would find her there for the first time again, squatting in the corner, nibbling nuts.

And I would see her, yes, once more. And she would raise her face, incomprehensible. And I, bewildered by her appearance, immediately overwhelmed by her presence, would invite her into another room, to that room with water and steam and mirrors, just to rest a little, to prolong a little what would happen, to breathe a little like before. I used to do it in that other time, the yesteryear, which all but ended right there and then.

And I would then return to my table, to my little mug of tea, to my way of imagining how sad all this was really going to be. How long. How useless. How dense.

The tea was already cold when she appeared in the doorway wrapped in a pure white towel. There were no longer bodies of steam swirling over the mug when she said:

"Spí uñieey mat."

Words like nuts in her dry mouth.

Spí Uñieey Mat

It's not a good idea to repeatedly ask yourself why you live in an estuary. Much less to do so in front of a mirror, probing yourself again and again. Why on earth? For what reason? With what purpose? It's likely you'll end up, sooner rather than later, with no answer at all. A gaping mouth. Blank eyes. The sky entirely filled with blue. After all, why do we live in any particular place? It must be the lack of an answer, that particular lack we feel when fruitlessly repeating the same question, that leads to responses such as this: "Because in estuaries you can find the coexistence of three types of photosynthesizing producers: macrophytes (algae, seagrasses, and marsh grasses); benthic microphytes (algae and other types of plants connected to the river bed); and phytoplankton (microscopic algae). That's why I live here, naturally." And then you feel the urge to open the cabin's window to look out once more on all this and confirm it. The word is *aestuarium*. It means "under the influence of the tides."

Staring at them, that's what I have been doing ever since I arrived.

Eyeing the tides, surreptitiously. Glancing at them without understanding much.

I am not a scientist. I didn't come to the estuary in search of ecological redemption. I wasn't born around here. Like others, I answered an ad printed in tiny letters for an attendant at a small museum on the edge of an estuary. To be more precise: on its banks. In the interview, I told them the truth: I had no great aspirations. But I didn't tell them the whole truth: I wanted to read. All I wanted was time to read. I thought this kind of job, with minimal responsibility and low expectations, would give me the necessary time to read a series of books I had added to an ever-growing list some years ago. I was filled with delight when I signed the contract, knowing that the meager salary and the absolute lack of expectations was supplemented with a place to live. A wooden cabin. A single bed. Some dishes. Two chairs. A refrigerator. I didn't think about anything the first time I witnessed through the window the low tides, under whose influence I still live. Pleasure is often like that.

Rocky coasts. Oyster reefs. Mangrove forests. River deltas. Beds of marine algae. Wooded marshes. I've seen all those images from so many other estuaries because they hang from the walls of the museum here. I've looked at them for countless hours, entire days. Dust-covered paintings. Black-and-white photographs. Stuffed and fading birds. I've spent so much time inspecting them that from the moment I come into the gallery I can tell which of the frames will require some adjustment. I've dedicated much of my energy and observational skills to this: to studying the frames from afar, approaching to straighten them, backing up again to see if the touch on the right or left side was enough, approaching them once again to make adjustments. This simple, almost mechanical operation has consumed many of my working hours. And because of that—because straightening frames and inspecting their details is what I do every day—when the first message appeared inscribed within one of the paintings, I couldn't believe it. *Ko'lew nñimát.* That's what it said. I didn't know anyone who could speak that language. I hadn't seen anyone in the museum write it.

Do you live in an estuary to find yourself permanently stuck within the words *mouth of the river*? Perhaps. The safest bet is that you live anywhere to go crazy or because you went crazy. I figured it was that and not something else that made me see tiny messages within the paintings of the estuary that later, when I tried to erase them, had already disappeared. Do you live in an estuary to read or to pretend that you read tiny messages in unknown languages? When I finally decided to investigate what those messages meant, I learned they belonged to a language in danger of extinction. My land, that's what it meant. Kiliwa, my land. Something like it, anyway. Needless to say, I don't come from that place.

I searched for the responsible party, of course. I pretended to read but really I spied. I trained my eyes in the ancient art of furtive observation. Without moving my head or gaze, without moving from my chair in the corner, I simply waited for the moment of apparition. And is that why, I would wonder at twilight, I live in an estuary? I studied them, yes. I studied them all the time. I studied the phrases: their advent and later their disappearance.

My search for the vandal distracted me from my habitual reading and, little by little, I abandoned my list of books. I already knew how to be quiet, but I gradually learned how to be even quieter. You stop speaking without realizing it. Later, over hours and days, you stop eating. But while your awareness grows, your questions don't go away: Why did I come to the estuary? What am I really doing here? My reaction to each question remains the same: I stand up to straighten one of the frames. Then I back up. I approach it again.

Spí uñieey mat.

The phrase appeared a long time ago. It was, in fact, one of the first I noticed. When it did, when it first appeared, it did so within a black-and-white photograph that fell to the floor, months later, due to the tremors of an earthquake. A tiny phrase at the bottom of a wooded marsh, that's what it was. Almost immediately I understood its meaning: *I don't want to die.* I still study it out of the corner of my eye. I still ask myself who left that message here. I still don't understand.

The Date

The investigation was all-consuming for seven months, but when she finally appeared it felt like it had taken a lifetime. He read newspapers and visited zoos, he showed up at the offices of various psychiatrists and veterinarians with invented ailments, and he slept in countless hotels. Finally, when he stopped the taxi and told the driver to take him to the Cosmos, he was almost certain she would be there. He gave himself a one percent margin of error. He told the hotel employee that he would like a large room, preferably on one of the top floors. "To have a better view of the whole city," he explained. Because it was the low season, he had no problem getting the presidential suite. It was just a little after six in the evening when he installed himself.

He noticed the smell almost as soon as he opened the door, but he restrained himself. When the bellhop left, he unfolded his clothing and hung it on the wooden hangers. He placed his toiletries in the bathroom: comb, creams, shaving brush. Then he retraced his steps and positioned himself before the window. The city was indeed at his feet. The evening light. The thin clouds. A firetruck sped down the narrow street but because the windows were made of soundproof glass, he couldn't hear the siren. A new Ulysses. From far away, as if they were tiny plastic dolls, men walked down the sidewalks. Men in suits and men in jeans. Men in rags. Men with hair and men without it. Men with crutches and men who slid through the crowd like eels. His sigh, discrete but forceful, seemed to belong to a man in love. Perhaps he was.

Then he took out his papers and placed them, in rigorous order, on the room's desk. He leafed through them as if he had never seen them before. There were all sorts of things there: notes scribbled in pencil and clippings from yellowing newspapers; photocopies that looked like old books as well as some recently printed pages; envelopes with foreign stamps and ancient recipes. It was a collage. A collection of clues and desires. He was just about to finish the task when someone knocked on the door. He jumped. A jolt of electricity shot up his spine. It seemed he was coming out of a long paralysis when he finally stood and walked toward the door. Before saying anything, he peered through the peephole. No one was there. When he opened the door, it was confirmed: all that was there was the hallway with its soft scarlet carpet and its walls covered in old gold paper. The tenuous light shining from the wall lamps only accentuated the absolute solitude of the passageway. At the tip of his shoes, just as he had sensed, was the closed envelope, white and rectangular, that contrasted with the geometric designs and color of the carpet. He opened it before closing the door: *Run away. Get out of this place. Soon you won't be able to escape.* The investigator smiled upon closing the door. A satisfied man.

It was after receiving the message that he picked up the telephone and ordered dinner to the room. Veal in a black apple sauce. Rabbit with artichokes and endives. Cenzontle liver pâté on slices of rye bread. Plum compote. Champagne. While waiting, he took out the tools from the second suitcase and placed them one by one on the dressing table. A drill. A screwdriver. Some tweezers. A hand saw. A measuring tape. A hammer. A mallet. Some nails. Some screws. A tiny army advancing in a straight line. When the dinner arrived, he threw everything back into the suitcase.

"So, you are visiting us for the first time?" the boy asked as he removed the crystal covers from the plates, allowing an aroma somewhere between sugary and aged to inundate the room.

The investigator told him that yes, he was.

"You made a peculiar selection," the waiter noted, looking at the dinner plates out of the corner of his eye. Then he smiled. His smile produced the same effect on the man's spine: a buzzing of racing ants against his bones. He was right then a statue. A chunk of stone from long ago. Something ripped from eternity. He was going to say something when the young man turned around. The carpet silenced his footsteps. Soft night noises. Then the man returned to his work.

He again pulled the tools from his suitcase and, with the drill in his right hand, he went over to the closet. It didn't take long to push aside the clothing he'd recently hung there. With his hands on the wood, feeling for holes with his bent knuckles, he found the opening. He was going to use the mallet when he realized there were new screws in the corners of the mahogany panel. He got his screwdriver. When he realized he needed the other one, he went back for the Phillips head. The sweat that dripped from his temples indicated he was in a rush. Little by little, the panel gave way. But before completely separating it from the wall, before introducing his head into the hole, he wiped away the sweat with a white handkerchief. Then he knelt down and leaned forward. With the help of his elbows, he slid into the other side of the closet.

He thought the information he'd obtained over so many months of investigation would prepare him for anything, but that wasn't the case. That is never the case. Imagination has its limits. He'd thought the cage would be big, which it was, but not that it would have the ancestral glamor of a boudoir. He'd imagined she would be bent over, like he'd read in so many journals, in a truly pre-human pose, but not that she would be swaying slowly, oh so slowly, from a swing made of fine metals. He had thought about her gaze a hundred times, imagining her with the dark eyes of the other woman, but nothing had prepared him for the prosaic sadness of the moment. The miniscule woman smiled, like the waiter had done before. And, when she signaled, by placing the tips of her fingers on her mouth, that she was hungry, he went back through the hole to bring the dinner plates one by one.

Then he amused himself by watching her eat while he savored the champagne.

"I thought you didn't exist," he said.

"That's right," she responded with a voice barely used to speaking.

My Voice in Sin Narrates

In the miserable game of mirror to mirror / my voice is falling / and my voice incinerates / and my voice in sin narrates / and my voice in sin elates
XAVIER VILLAURRUTIA, NOCTURNE: NOTHING IS HEARD, TR. ELIOT WEINBERGER

I couldn't see the road; I heard the voice.

The voice and the drum. The voice that failed, and the drum that survived. The voice that tried again, only to fail again. The drum: indefatigable. The hypnosis generated by the rhythm of trial and error. One after another. And another one. And after. Something without mercy. Trial and error: the incessant repetition. A rhythm. A fascination. An infinite number of singers and an unlimited number of percussionists. A piece by Cardew. Communal music.

I couldn't see the road; I breathed in the aroma of her presence.

The skin and the perfume. The skin, so close; and the perfume, inconceivable. Amber both: the skin and the scent. The fragrance, definitely a woman's, and her skin, on a body that drove in total concentration under the fleeting shade of the oyameles. An orange light all around, incinerating. The light of the wildfire. The smoke.

"Is that Cardew?" I asked, my eyes still closed.

She didn't answer right away. Before saying anything, she looked insistently at the rearview mirror and the side mirror, checking how much time we had.

"A piece by Cardew, remember?" she said, as if we were on a weekend stroll. "The Great Learning," she added in a very low voice, a voice willing to become inaudible. The voice that fails, and the drums. The voice that catches fire and, as the fallen leaves or the parched grass, as the bushes and the canopies of trees, is frantically reduced to ash. The voice that incinerates. The drums.

I couldn't see the road; I felt the burning in my throat, my temples feverish, the pain on the back of the neck. Allergies. Asthma. What else? The dust and the debris settled in the airways of my lungs and forced me to cough over and over again until I bent down, only to fall once more onto the back—now almost horizontal—of the car seat. A failure. I didn't see the road but I listened to what she was describing in manic detail. She depicted the narrow strip we traveled on, barely two lanes, bordered by tall oyameles and deep ravines. "Very deep," she clarified. She spoke of the flock of birds, fleeing and failing to flee. Catching fire instead. The flames, leaping from tree top to tree top. A series of firebrands. The slow mammals crossing the road. A pair of crazed chickens. The smoke, billowing. She described the afternoon light, an orange glow about to turn yellow again, then, perhaps, colorless, as it pierced through the dense branches of the forest trees, wounding them. Leaving them for dead.

"The forest was once so lovely," she also said, although it would have been more accurate to describe her use of words as murmuring or babbling. "We'll get out of here, you'll see. We'll get out of the forest," she insisted, repeating it many times, failing to convince even herself. A failure. Another one. The beat of the drums.

We were going down a narrow road at full speed, that much was clear. And she couldn't help it. If I opened my eyes, the heat and the smoke would hurt my pupils, setting off a river of tears. Brackish drops. Painless drops. If I sat up straight, the coughing would return immediately. If I spoke, if I tried to utter more than three words in a row, the pressure in the center of my chest became unbearable. We were going down a narrow road, a dangerous road full of holes and loose rocks, a road that was actually closed, under repair, or completely forgotten, and there was nothing we could do but babble and lie down as we listened to the many echoing, varied ways Cardew's voices died. The voices of the great learning.

I couldn't see the road; I heard her voice. Her voice said that she would never have imagined that, at the end of it all, she would find herself driving a car at full speed while describing, in awkward nervous gibbering, the winter light and the way it pierced through the limbs of the tall oyameles, ripping them apart. Burning, the voice. Its ring. The way it resembled the drums, incinerating.

"If someone would have predicted this, say at a village fair or in a Turkish cafe with tiny round tables, filled with the smoke of many cigars, I would have thought that the gypsy or fortune teller was just a crazy charlatan," she continued in a whisper, looking at the rearview mirror, the side mirror. How much time was left? Her inner alarm setting off. Her attempt at control.

"I remember," I whispered, "I remember Cardew."

If someone had glanced at us from afar, from above, from the open window of a helicopter, for example, the vision could have been divine. The wildfire barely behind us, devastating the forest as it sprawled endlessly, hot on our heels. A sacred spring and, then, around it, a forest haunted by flames and smoke: the story of a life as the story of a moment. The fire, imprinting its color on rock, ravine, pine tree, cloud. The compact white car she moved forward. A kind of rocket. Definitely toward. The image: it could be a television advertisement, a spectacular ad about the end of the world. You are here. You were always here. The compact car, and us in it, striving for a lake or the sea. An unknown forward.

"What?" she asked as she rounded a curve, slowing down at the same time. "What did you just say?" she insisted when she heard no response.

I couldn't see the road; I crouched over with a new fit of coughing. Her hand on my left knee. Her compassion. And the ghostly voices assembled by Cardew. And the crazed drums. And the book of Confucius. And the amazement. And your control. All yours.

"There's still some water left in the bottle, I think," she said, and reached for it with her right arm behind my seat, keeping her left hand on the steering wheel and her eyes on the windshield and her foot on the gas.

The water tasted like clay to me. Water from a well. Water that has been in touch with the earth, one with the mud. Healing water. A sip.

"Would you have imagined this?"

I shook my head.

"I would have told the fortune teller that she was a charlatan on the spot, just like that, with those very words. You are a charlatan. You see? It's not that difficult."

It was her same old voice. A voice unmistakably hers: firm and ironic and yet complacent. It was undoubtedly a kind voice. A voice that, mature, burning, full of ashes, that turning all into ashes, filled the interior space of the car with something akin to eternity. A voice that incinerates. Something serene and complete and with no way out. I shivered. A voice in sin. A voice narrates.

"I wouldn't have believed her either," I finally said out loud, holding back my cough as I attempted a smile.

The silence told me that she had smiled at herself too, pleased. She still liked to be right. I opened my left eye and confirmed my suspicion: I lay down next to a smiling woman. A satisfied woman searching for her own eyes in the rearview mirror, and then in the side mirror. How many minutes? I thought it had been so easy after all. I thought that, at the end of it all, it had been quite simple. A blaze, swirls of deep gray smoke on the horizon, and a smiling woman. I closed the eye that was beginning to water and barely caressed the hand that she kept on the gear stick.

"And you came to the spring to save yourself?" she asked, feeling it now: my hand on hers, almost weightless: on safe ground, or at least no longer threatening. There was no mockery in her voice, but curiosity. A bit of disbelief. "Why else would people come to sacred springs," she answered herself.

I couldn't see the road but smelled the scorching earth. I barely breathed in. Breathed out. I coughed. How many seconds left? The flames reached upward, embracing the sky. Embracing Cardew.

"I assumed you've been like this for a long time," she said while I stooped over again, trying to clear my lungs. "I suppose you were also taken aback when the fire walked, like Jesus Christ, on the water," she said, stepping on the gas.

I answered her questions, which she enumerated slowly, leaving space between them so that the silence would allow me to picture the forest: the blaze: the blistering landscape, the flames, with grunts, sighs, slight movements of hands and head, unable as I was to say something aloud without coughing. I assumed that she had come to the sacred spring for reasons we shared. For we did believe, I wanted to shout out but couldn't. We believed, didn't we? The whooping began again. The car hit a bump and the sudden movement of the vehicle stopped the sound of the music.

I didn't see the road, but imagined the mountains she described. The spectacular rocks. The deep texture of the trunks. The variations of the green that, being winter, decayed into either black or nothing. The blond grass. I breathed in her scent, our belief. I brushed, with great difficulty, almost fearfully, her right hand.

"Looks like we're going on a picnic," she said, barely containing a self-deprecating grin, which was exactly what I was thinking at the time.

"If someone saw us right now, they'd think we were happy." She lowered her voice, trying to prevent me from hearing how it splintered. How it splattered against the windshield, falling apart. How it caught on fire and, then, how it raced through time, incinerating itself. Becoming nothing but ashes.

"That we were happy," she said, correcting herself, reclaiming her poise.

"If someone other than us," she said again. "If a pair of strangers glanced at us right now from afar, I mean," she insisted. "They wouldn't know, would they?"

I attempted a smile and failed. The drums. The maddening rhythm of the drums and the humming speed of the car. I imagined that I looked like a satisfied woman myself, touching her hand as if patting a domesticated animal. The music returned. The car dodged a couple of medium-sized rocks, but the sharp turn caused me to hit my head on the window.

"We will run out of gas soon," she whispered. "We are going to have to stop and open the doors and set foot on the land," she said, calmly, enumerating our actions one by one. A well-organized parade. A gymnastics routine. "We will have to find our way through the woods," she said. "We will."

I couldn't see the road; I felt the burning behind my eyelids and heard, like a spectral drum, like a wretched little drum that kept beating inside the cavity of my own chest, the noise kindled by the scandalous contact between the drops of her sweat and the luminous skin on her cheek, her neck, her clavicles. We believed, didn't we? I wanted to say. The voice that narrates. The sin. We visited a sacred spring and smelled, quite by chance, the earth's perfume.

TRANSLATED BY THE AUTHOR

Revenge

I came to the camps because I was bored. The electricity was out at home again and the only thing left was the usual: listen to the adults ranting or light a candle to read a tattered magazine. I'd run out of candles, so, with my coat on my back, I went out into the street.

I had seen them before, of course. They settled during the spring on the side of the hill, under a large jacaranda tree. No one said anything, mostly because they minded their own business and were impeccably clean. After clearing a vacant lot to pitch their tents, and before going to work on their vegetable gardens, they set up clotheslines between the still-standing trees. What they needed to dispose of, which was really very little, they sold at recycling centers. That's what I learned the day I went down to sell a whole box full of empty beer cans.

"You drank quite a bit yesterday, didn't you?" said one of the residents of the camps, half joking. His eyes were owl-colored and that's why I answered him.

"No way," I murmured with a little laugh, looking down. "I collected them over months. Maybe a year."

The accumulation of the cans piqued his interest, I suppose, because he followed me up the hill and all the way to the door of my house.

"This is where they found a corpse yesterday, right?" He was pointing to a spot on the street just a few feet away from us.

I nodded.

"A clean shot in the back of the neck, right?" he asked, though he was really just confirming what he already knew. "His forehead on the steering wheel."

"Yes," I said lowering my voice, and then, looking fearfully at the windows across the street, I couldn't say more.

"I got it," he said, glancing around cautiously. And then he held out his hand. I stared at his hand for a while not really knowing what to do. Shaking a hand: what an antiquated gesture.

"Comrade," he finally declared. A big smile on his lips. I had never heard that word before.

The next time I saw him he gave me a white blouse.

"It's made of natural cotton," he said, quite enthusiastically. "So, you won't have to wear those dresses that kill the earth," he added when I looked him in the eye, hesitating before the gift.

I turned to look down at my clothes: a pair of old jeans, a ragged t-shirt, my white panties, a lousy bra. All deadly. I smiled. The blouse looked more like a burlap sack, but it fit me well. In fact, it was the one I was wearing the night I grabbed my coat and left the house in such a hurry, as if running for my life. Rage didn't motivate me, and even now I don't know what hope is, but I was sick to death of the routine. The same family drama every day. The same thing over and over, every day. The whining. The defeat. The resignation. The whining all over again. My sprint was short-lived. I slowed down as soon as I made out the shadows of the soldiers in the neighborhood. I was surprised to see the military checkpoint. They were all over the city, of course, but usually a little farther south, near the paved streets. Who would be interested in guarding us, perched on the sides of the hills? I was surprised by the deafening sound of helicopter blades, hovering right overhead. I imagined the worst. I assumed that another corpse or many corpses had been found. More executions. But I didn't see anything. I stopped. I scanned the area. Instead of stopping me or asking me for my papers, the soldiers ordered me to move on. When I did, I couldn't help but take one last look. I twisted around, little by little, trying to face what I was leaving behind. There was once a woman who did the same thing, and she became a legend. I only managed to see the banners hanging from the trees, featuring the word REVENGE in large red letters. I mumbled it several times, that word. I uttered it with care, salivating. I repeated it in a very low voice every time the heel of my shoes hit the pebbles and the dirt road. Revenge. Then I remembered the festivities. Very recently, the government had organized a celebration of some sort in the paved area of the city, on the other side of town. There was plenty of dirty confetti in the mud of our neighborhood. Something like the aroma of fried food wafted through the air. A colorful streamer tangled around my ankle.

I stopped to look at it all from the top of the hill, brooding. At night, lit by hundreds of street lamps, the city is a swarm of fireflies. I like that word: fireflies. I looked it up in the dictionary and then I found an image on the internet. Stunning, really, the word fireflies, which lights up. By day, the city is something else entirely. By day, the swarm is gray and what darts over the houses and through streets are nothing more than flies and cockroaches. Seagulls, which are birds of prey. The helicopters and their blades. There, not far away, you can see the four border walls that, one behind the other, frame our lockdown. I guess we are locked in here. I guess we really won't ever get out.

Maybe it was a sudden fit of claustrophobia or plain old boredom, but I charged on. I decided I wouldn't stop until I reached the camps. The decision seemed to cheer me up because, despite gasping for air, I got back to my initial speed. All the shops were closed, even the bakeries. No lines in front of the water supplies stalls. I tripped a couple of times over rocks and feared I would fall. I didn't. It's hard to fall, after all. I scurried fast in front of buildings and houses and like a shadow through vacant lots. I guess that's what I was. A shadow. The shadow of a shadow. The cats and dogs looked at me sideways. Scared or amused, who knows. Who cares. The shadow, in any case, stopped in her tracks before I did. The shadow understood it immediately, long before I could even spot the jacaranda, the clotheslines, the tents. And she was rendered speechless. Their bodies formed a strange map on the surface of the earth. Their bodies. His hands. All those bones.

I ran away, naturally. The soldiers and the dogs and the neighbors across the street watched my steps suspiciously but motionless. Were they expecting something? I went home with the good news that the government had temporarily suspended the rationing during the festivities. Were they still expecting something? "We can watch television," I said. And the children cheered, relieved. My mother stared at me, unable to decide whether or not I was lying. The kids hurled themselves onto the only sofa all at once, fighting over the remote until they realized it was useless. There was only one program on every channel. "No way," they said in disbelief. Whining. "This is it," my father howled, in defeat. "Come on, help me peel these potatoes," my mother said, resigned. I stood in front of the screen. When I moved away from the campsites, I had managed to get a glimpse of the back of their shoulders, their muffled hair, the napes of their necks. I couldn't see anything else. A man in a tuxedo smiled on the screen, facing me. His bright white teeth. His gelled hair. "We're counting on you," he announced, raising his index finger. "The future," he said. The glow of the television illuminated the camps once again: their broken hands, their foreheads, their innocent garments. "We count on you," he insisted.

And Lot's wife finally turned her back on all of it.

TRANSLATED BY THE AUTHOR

Two Nameless Women

I could hear the water running as I inserted the key in the lock. I thought I'd find her right where she was: in the tiny bathroom, sitting on the edge of the bathtub, with her hands still under the stream of hot water. She was staring at something I wasn't able to make out through the window. She was looking at it insistently. She only realized I was there when I turned off the faucet and hurriedly placed the dry towel on her warm red hands.

"Look what you've done," I murmured, trying to reprimand her. "They look like newly plucked chickens," I finally smiled, caressing them. She looked at me with her empty eyes. Then she blinked and, bending her head, looked at her hands. She lifted the right one up to her eyes, rotating it to better inspect it.

"Their hands," she said. "They cut their hands."

"Yes," I answered as I gently pushed her toward her room. After turning off the television, I helped her sit down on her bed to take off her clothes, baggy pants and a cotton t-shirt, and put on the flannel nightgown she slept in. She motioned for me to pass her the brush sitting on the dresser and, as soon as she held it in her hands, she devoted herself to running it through her long gray hair. She seemed absorbed once again. The brush easily glided from the roots to the tips and then did so once more.

"This time they also cut their legs," she murmured, suddenly looking at me.

"Yes," I answered her. "I saw on the news. We'll have to be more careful from now on," I concluded, giving her a few pats on the back and offering her a couple pills. Then I went to the little kitchen and put water on to boil. Time passes in strange ways. When the kettle emitted its high-pitched sound, a sound that always reminds me of a police siren, I had no idea what I'd been thinking about. I made her an orange blossom tea because I knew it was one of her favorites.

"And they cut their hair, too," she said as if to herself when she took her first sip with unusual calm. She turned to look at me, and, knowing I was being looked at, I smiled at her. I never quite know what to do in these situations. When I turned off the bedroom light, the old woman was already asleep under the blankets. Her breathing, measured. Her eyelashes, still.

The building where we lived was gloomy, certainly, but it had the advantage of being centrally located. We could manage quite easily without a car, riding the bus or the subway when I needed to take her to the hospital for her routine check-ups. There were plenty of restaurants nearby where we could pick up food without an additional fee. There were laundromats and a post office and a police station. And I could see all this from the windows of her fourth floor. The red lights. The traffic lights.

That night I sat a while in her favorite armchair before ending my daily visit. I didn't know for sure how she spent her days, all by herself, locked in the labyrinth of her own head, but I could read her activities in the traces she left behind: the television on, the door of the refrigerator open, a couples of knives on the counter. Her family had all but forgotten her, visiting her every now and then, especially on her birthday. She received a card or two throughout the year. A letter. I looked out the window just like I had seen her frequently do. The city outside trembled. It gave off that impression, anyway. I placed my legs on the ottoman and leaned back against the headrest. The cracks in the ceiling formed a map or a forest of twisted trees or a fishing net where a prisoner would have to fall. I closed my eyes, like the old woman, and thought that I was perhaps as exhausted as she was. Or as lost. Is it really necessary to live so long? I opened my eyes and crossed myself before even standing up. In the darkness, the apartment looked like a little museum of itself. The photographs. The rugs. The curtains. The spoons and forks. The vases. The wallpaper. Every object had been carefully preserved. No touching. The table. The chairs. I couldn't help but wonder who would wind up with all this in the end. I picked up the plastic bag in which I was carrying a loaf of bread and slices of ham for a sandwich. After taking a final look at the apartment, I left and locked the door. I slowly walked down the stairs to the second floor. How long is eternity, measured in steps?

On the television they kept showing the same news. The dead girls. The signs of torture. The lingering question about their names. I avoided looking at the images, but I listened to them recount the events from the kitchen: a party gone wrong, a taxi, a ride into eternity. The police sirens interrupted my thoughts. The boiling water. As I spread the mayonnaise on the bread, I imagined the blue sky over their bodies. The sunlight, vertical, spade-like over their skin. The sunlight when it collides with bones. Their mouths, open. All those precious teeth. I fell into a chair. I looked at the wall. With the knife still in my right hand, inert like the statue I already was, I thought about how they hadn't even had the time to feel tired. I thought about how, had they been saved, had they survived, they could rest their legs on the thick leather of the ottoman in the middle of a lonesome room.

Rothko's Sunrise

What the bird observes through the window:
There is a man placing articles of clothing in a big suitcase. Little by little, at a regular rhythm, the man slides with certain slowness from the foot of the bed, where all the garments are scattered, toward the closet, at the bottom of which the bag is wide open. The man takes the same route over and over: a lunar orbit. He does it methodically, without looking up. Walking: one foot in front of the other. There is also a woman, but she is sitting on the bed pillows, her back against the wall. On her legs crossed in a lotus position rests a book that she reads out loud. A floor lamp to her right. A lamp turned on.

The bird cocks its head as if reacting to the words it cannot hear from the other side of the glass. The opening and closing of its eyelids. The dark night. So dark. If this were the bird that visited the window in a DeLillo novel, surely it would be warbling the words "impossible realms." The light the room's window emits barely illuminates a solitary oak-lined street.

—

What the nocturnal ambler observes:
A bird that sings at night. How strange. There is a bird that sings at night.

What the woman observes when she closes the book and says nothing more:
The man has collapsed in the middle of a springy armchair, his back to the window through which a black bird spies on the room. Shrunken by the size of the chair, the man appears more exhausted than he is. His arms fallen to the sides of his body. His eyes open. His forehead implacable. The woman surely imagines a hat on top of that head of short blonde hair. She thinks, this too with utmost certainty: he is a tormented man. A man from a long time ago, another century, even. Someone who does not know.

What the man observes within his head:
If she were to read the poem, she would do it out loud. Reading is sometimes escaping. The bird would hear the echo: *You want to get out, you want to tear yourself out, I am the outside, I am snow.* And outside, then, it would be snowing. The night suddenly turned into a pure white shroud upon contact with the voice. *Wrenching your way through,* she would continue, stumbling. *This is urgent,* she would snap the book closed then, and he, from the armchair, fighting against an infinite tiredness, would demand she continue. His eyes open. *It's your life,* she would mur-

mur in an increasingly quiet tone, embarrassed. *Last chance for freedom.*

What the author of the poem observes from the window of her studio far from there, somewhere else:
A couple of children play with snowballs. They laugh, she can tell by the gestures on their faces, though the laughter does not pierce the glass. Their bodies leave marks on the snow that quickly disappear. Tabula rasa.

What the man observes from the bed (retrospective):
The bird looks at him curiously from the entangled branch of an oak tree. Black on black. The wrinkles his body pulled forth from the fabric of the armchair have been erased. No one has been there, mulling things over. *To weigh* means to lift something so as to discover its importance or to recognize it. No one there heard the sounds of the words that made him smile as he slowly stood, as if he were older or heavier. This: a body that trudges through time. No one avoided looking back: the face under the shroud of the snow. No one.

What the man observes from the bed (prospective):
The feet, under the gray blankets, form precipitous little mountains. The knees. The hips. He remembers the words and sees the letters floating in the room's warm air. To breathe is a movement. The ceiling, without any cracks, a tabula rasa made of snow. When he leans over her head, like the bird did before the scene

of the two of them, he wonders about her dreams. He warbles: impossible realms. A thread of saliva on her chin. How strange. There is a bird that sings at night. The lipstick stains on the edges of the pillows. Impressionism. Her hair: strands in the shape of question marks. The shoulder blade is an optical chimera.

The man, his right hand on the woman's shoulder, finally closes his eyes.

What no one sees:
It is a stupendous sunrise. The light slowly emerges along the edges of the visible world until it spills, delicately, over the middle of everything. Iridescent. The trees acquire form. A branch is a branch. The trunks. The trembling multitude of leaves. Said about a bird, *to flap* means to frequently move the wings without flying off. Said about a man, it means to move the arms like wings. In the rectangle of the window, which is made up of two clearly differentiated squares, the color red settles in. The process of impregnation. It is just a moment, nothing more. The bird suddenly takes flight. *To flap* also means to catch your breath.

Rothko's Sunrise: Told in Six Narrative Villanelles, Eight Poker Cards, and Some Loose Lines

I: WHAT THE BIRD OBSERVES THROUGH THE WINDOW:
There is a man placing articles of clothing in a big suitcase.
Little by little, at a regular rhythm, the man slides with certain slowness from the foot of the bed, where all the garments are scattered, toward the closet, at the bottom of which the bag is wide open.
The man takes the same route over and over: a lunar orbit.

He does it methodically, without looking up.
Walking: one foot in front of the other.
There is a man placing articles of clothing in a big suitcase.

There is also a woman, but she is sitting on the bed pillows, her back against the wall.
On her legs, crossed in a lotus position, rests a book that she reads out loud.
The man takes the same route over and over: a lunar orbit.

A floor lamp to her right.

A lamp turned on.
There is a man placing articles of clothing in a big suitcase.

The bird cocks its head as if reacting to the words it cannot hear
from the other side of the glass.
The opening and closing of its eyelids.
The man takes the same route over and over: a lunar orbit.

The dark night. So dark.
If this were the bird that visited the window in a DeLillo novel,
surely it would be warbling the words "impossible realms."
There is a man placing articles of clothing in a big suitcase.
The man takes the same route over and over: a lunar orbit.

The light the room's window emits barely illuminates a solitary oak-lined street.

II: WHAT THE NOCTURNAL AMBLER OBSERVES:
A bird that sings at night.
How strange.
There is a bird that sings at night.

♠

III: WHAT THE WOMAN OBSERVES WHEN SHE CLOSES THE BOOK
AND SAYS NOTHING MORE:
The man has collapsed in the middle of a springy armchair, his back

to the window through which a black bird spies on the room.
Shrunken by the size of the chair, the man appears more exhausted
than he is.
His arms fallen to the sides of his body.
His eyes open.

His forehead implacable.
The woman surely imagines a hat on top of that head of short
blonde hair.
The man has collapsed in the middle of a springy armchair, his back
to the window through which a black bird spies on the room.

She thinks, this too with utmost certainty: he is a tormented man.
A man from a long time ago, another century, even.
His eyes open.

Someone who does not know.

IV: WHAT THE MAN OBSERVES WITHIN HIS HEAD:
The man has collapsed in the middle of a spring armchair, his back
to the window through which a black bird spies on the room.

If she were to read the poem, she would do it out loud.
Reading is sometimes escaping.
His eyes open.

The bird would hear the echo: *You want to get out, you want to
tear yourself out, I am the outside, I am snow.*

And outside, then, it would be snowing.
The man has collapsed in the middle of a springy armchair, his back to the window through which a black bird spies on the room.
His eyes open.

The night suddenly converted into a pure white shroud upon contact with the voice. *Wrenching your way through*, she would continue, stumbling.
This is urgent, she would snap the book closed then, and he, from the armchair, fighting against an infinite tiredness, would demand she continue.

His eyes open.
It's your life, she would murmur in an increasingly quiet tone, embarrassed.
The night suddenly converted into a pure white shroud upon contact with the voice.

Last chance for freedom.

V: WHAT THE AUTHOR OF THE POEM OBSERVES FROM THE WINDOW OF HER STUDIO FAR FROM THERE, SOMEWHERE ELSE:
This is urgent, she would snap the book closed then, and he, from the armchair, fighting against an infinite tiredness, would demand she continue.

A couple of children play with snowballs.

They laugh, he can tell by the gestures on their faces, though the laughter does not pierce the glass.
The night suddenly converted into a pure white shroud upon contact with the voice.

Their bodies leave marks on the snow that quickly disappear. Tabula rasa.
This is urgent, she would snap the book closed then, and he, from the armchair, fighting against an infinite tiredness, would demand she continue.

VI: WHAT THE MAN OBSERVES FROM THE BED (RETROSPECTIVE):
The bird looks at him curiously from the entangled branch of an oak tree.
The night suddenly converted into a pure white shroud upon contact with the voice.
This is urgent, she would snap the book closed then, and he, from the armchair, fighting against an infinite tiredness, would demand she continue.

◆

Black on black.
The wrinkles his body pulled forth from the fabric of the armchair have been erased.
No one has been there, mulling things over.

To weigh means to lift something so as to discover its importance or to recognize it.

No one heard there the sounds of the words that made him smile as he slowly stood, as if he were older or heavier.
Black on black.

This: a body that trudges through time.
No one avoided looking back: the face under the shroud of the snow.
No one has been there, mulling things over.

No one.

VII: WHAT THE MAN OBSERVES FROM THE BED (PROSPECTIVE):
Black on black.

The feet, under the gray blankets, form precipitous little mountains.
The knees.
No one has been there, mulling things over.

The hips.
He remembers the words and sees the letters floating in the room's warm air.
Black on black.
No one has been there, mulling things over.

He remembers the words and sees the letters floating in the room's warm air.

To breathe is a movement.
The ceiling, without any cracks, a tabula rasa made of snow.

There is a bird that sings at night.
The lipstick stains on the edges of the pillows.
He remembers the words and sees the letters floating in the room's warm air.

Impressionism.
Her hair: strands in the shape of question marks.
The ceiling, without any cracks, a tabula rasa made of snow.

The shoulder blade is an optical chimera.
The man, his right hand on the woman's shoulder, finally closes his eyes.
He remembers the words and sees the letters floating in the room's warm air.
The ceiling, without any cracks, a tabula rasa made of snow.

♠

VIII: WHAT NO ONE SEES:
It is a stupendous sunrise.
The light slowly emerges along the edges of the visible world until it spills, delicately, over the middle of everything.

Iridescent.
The trees acquire form.

VIII: WHAT NO ONE SEES:

A branch is a branch.

The trunks.

The light slowly emerges along the edges of the visible world until it spills, still delicately, over the middle of everything.

The trembling multitude of leaves.

Said about a bird, *to flap* means to frequently move the wings without flying off.

VIII: WHAT NO ONE SEES:

Said about a man, it means to move the arms like wings.

In the rectangle of the window, which is made up of two clearly differentiated squares, the color red settles in.

The light slowly emerges along the edges of the visible world until it spills, still delicately, over the middle of everything.

The process of impregnation.

It is just a moment, nothing more.

VIII: WHAT NO ONE SEES:

The light slowly emerges along the edges of the visible world until it spills, still delicately, over the middle of everything.

The bird suddenly takes flight. *To flap* also means to catch your breath.

The Survivor from Pripyat

(Record A)

Lutavia arrived from Google on "NO HAY TAL LUGAR" 16/06/2010 by searching for <u>Women from the Highlands who once crossed the Pripyat River in absolute silence</u> 11:37:42—13 hours 43 minutes ago.

Lutavia arrived from Google on "NO HAY TAL LUGAR" 23/07/2010 by searching for <u>What do you do when you find a moose beyond the helm of the ferry that slowly crosses the Pripyat River?</u> 11:45:32—12 hours 32 minutes ago.

Tijuana arrived from Google on "NO HAY TAL LUGAR 03/01/2004–04/01/2004" 24/07/2010 by searching for <u>Lutavia stops</u> 09:39:14—12 minutes ago.

Lutavia arrived from Google on "NO HAY TAL LUGAR" 25/07/2010 by searching for <u>There is a man who floats on the</u>

waters of the Pripyat River naked, his arms outstretched, his eyes wide-open. The infinite, ah 11:15:48—11 hours 23 minutes ago.

Lutavia arrived from Google on "NO HAY TAL LUGAR" 25/07/2010 by searching for The nuclear horses still gallop among the rusted, inert machines, under the branches of the days, this spasm 11:23:12—11 hours 31 minutes ago.

Lutavia arrived from Google on "NO HAY TAL LUGAR" 25/07/2010 by searching for Look, this is the wheel of fortune. These are the dolls with which you played. Here, in this empty room, a tree grows 11:29:17—11 hours 37 minutes ago.

Lutavia arrived from Google on "NO HAY TAL LUGAR" 25/07/2010 by searching for But autumn will come—you know?— and I will proceed among the excessively tall sprigs with this shield and with this scepter 11:30:23—11 hours 38 minutes ago.

Tijuana arrived from Google on "NO HAY TAL LUGAR" 16/08/2010 by searching for The survivor from Pripyat who crosses the river again and again, again and again, does not exist 8:54:04—12 minutes ago.

Lutavia arrived from Google on "NO HAY TAL LUGAR" 17/08/2010 by searching for The sniper among the weeds. The horse-devourer. Someone eats and vomits and defecates. This is existence 11:12:56—10 hours 21 minutes ago.

—

Lutavia arrived from Google on "NO HAY TAL LUGAR" 18/08/2010 by searching for <u>The rotting teeth. Gnawed fingernails. Calluses on the soles of the feet. Scars on the torso and arms. The body enveloped in radium, thorium, uranium. This is existence</u> 10:54:13—11 hours 43 minutes ago.

Lutavia arrived from Google on "NO HAY TAL LUGAR" 23/08/2010 by searching for <u>And what story isn't a handful of phrases inside a search engine?</u> 11:13:12—10 hours 03 minutes ago.

Tijuana arrived from Google on "NO HAY TAL LUGAR" 24/08/2010 by searching for <u>I swear I read the story of the survivor from Pripyat. I swear I believe it</u> 5:12:16—03 minutes ago.

Lutavia arrived from Google on "NO HAY TAL LUGAR" 25/08/2010 by searching for <u>What raspberry tastes like on the tongue. How you touch the skin of a stuffed horse. The sound of boots in the weeds</u> 11:34:45—7 hours 43 minute ago.

Lutavia arrived from Google on "NO HAY TAL LUGAR" 01/09/2010 by searching for <u>It has to do with stretching your muscles and letting yourself go. It has to do with opening your eyes and your hands and your skin and your fingernails. This is the water that beholds</u> 11:36:19—10 hours 43 minutes ago.

Lutavia arrived from Google on "NO HAY TAL LUGAR" 02/09/2010 by searching for <u>Submerge yourself for the last time. Turn on a forty-watt lightbulb. Chew. Swallow. Drink. Type. This is existence</u> 10:03:12—9 hours 23 minutes ago.

Tijuana arrived from Google on "NO HAY TAL LUGAR" 19/09/2010 by searching for <u>And at what moment Lutavia? At what moment does the water in the river freeze? How do you get by unnoticed?</u> 5:13:13—12 minutes ago.

Lutavia arrived from Google on "NO HAY TAL LUGAR" 30/12/2010 by searching for <u>"I hoped everything would stay behind. Erased or crossed out forever. I hoped. But nothing, not even the bird, vanished." I am about to weigh anchor</u> 11:48:33—9 hours 07 minutes ago.

Lutavia arrived from Google on "NO HAY TAL LUGAR" 01/01/2011 by searching for <u>The moose and later the eagles arrived. The silence of the snow is spectacular. There should be a search for tubers. Wish you were here is written on the front of postcards from Pripyat</u> 11:34:32—10 hours 24 minutes ago.

Lutavia arrived from Google on "NO HAY TAL LUGAR" 02/01/2011 by searching for <u>The foot that breaks. The way the body falls on the snow. The print that remains. And here</u> 11:45:09—9 hours 14 minutes ago.

Lutavia arrived from Google on "NO HAY TAL LUGAR" 15/01/2011 by searching for There is a hungry man. There is a hand missing two fingers. A few days ago a pack of hyenas or dogs passed through here 11:12:11—10 hours 37 minutes ago.

Lutavia arrived from Google on "NO HAY TAL LUGAR" 23/01/2011 by searching for Thirst is perhaps the worst. Thirst and salt. Acetylsalicylic acid. The sound of the ice when it cracks in two 11:21:45—8 hours 49 minutes ago.

Tijuana arrived from Google on "NO HAY TAL LUGAR" 24/01/2011 by searching for The writing is radioactive, this we know. Cesium. Thorium. Uranium. The river doesn't exist. You don't either, Pripyat 8:32:12—23 minutes ago.

Lutavia arrived from Google on "NO HAY TAL LUGAR" 24/01/2011 by searching for My hand. My waste. My perpendicular. What's a book but an isolation zone, the perimeter that must be guarded thirty kilometers around? 10:32:41—9 hours 26 minutes ago.

Lutavia arrived from Google on "NO HAY TAL LUGAR" 24/01/2011 by searching for What is a book but a way of imagining what lies, moribund, on the other side of the screen? Or a way of grabbing onto the edge of the roof or the last gasp of air? 10:37:34—9 hours 28 minutes ago.

Lutavia arrived from Google on "NO HAY TAL LUGAR" 25/01/2011 by searching for <u>You have to look for the true book in the residues, in the corners, in the most hidden places. This is the trace that disappears</u> 11:01:34—10 hours 23 minutes ago.

Tijuana arrived from Google on "NO HAY TAL LUGAR" 28/01/2011 by searching for <u>We need a doctor. Maybe two</u> 5:15:23—03 minutes ago.

Lutavia arrived from Google on "NO HAY TAL LUGAR" 12/02/2011 by searching for <u>Otherwise, if it has been conceived then it is real. If it is real, then it can die</u> 11:12:17—10 hours 34 minutes ago.

Lutavia arrived from Google on "NO HAY TAL LUGAR" 21/03/2011 by searching for <u>This is the moment you dream about a moose. Now the horses pass over the steppe, illuminated. Look, here. On this line. This is the moment you wake up</u> 11:27:12—10 hours 21 minutes ago.

(Record B)
The first time he visited my page:
Lutavia arrived from Google on "NO HAY TAL LUGAR" 16/06/2010 by searching for <u>Women from the Highlands who once crossed the Pripyat River in absolute silence</u> 11:37:42—13 hours 43 minutes ago.

It would have gone completely unnoticed if it hadn't happened a second time:

Lutavia arrived from Google on "NO HAY TAL LUGAR" 23/07/2010 by searching for <u>What do you do when you find a moose beyond the helm of the ferry that slowly crosses the Pripyat River?</u> 11:45:32—12 hours 32 minutes ago.

The phrases that guided their search were too long to ignore. That was true from the beginning. And it didn't take long for me to realize that all of them, at least in the early records, were indiscreetly related to a story I had written long ago. *Strange is the Bird that Can Cross the River Pripyat.* My portrait of the Apocalypse— which is any relationship between an Old Man, a Girl, and a Little Boy—with a little electronica music and frozen temperatures. But the other mystery, the central mystery, in fact, was that up until that moment I had thought that Lutavia, the place from which these visits were generated, was a destination I had invented years before. On March 9, 2004, as documented on www.cristinariveragarza.blogspot.com, I wrote about this tiny northern republic where snow always falls for the first time. That it existed, moreover, that this term would appear alongside a lavender-colored flag with a purple border replete with little yellow stars, a large black hole in the center, left me reflecting for days. So this is real? As far as I knew, I had never offered raspberry candies to anyone ("Reclusive by nature [they say the snow makes them like that], the only way of extracting information from a Lutavian is to offer them raspberry candies") and I had never heard anyone speak the most secret of languages, which is how Lutavanese is usually described.

Lutavia arrived from Google on "NO HAY TAL LUGAR" 25/07/2010 by searching for <u>There is a man who floats on the waters of the Pripyat River naked, his arms outstretched, his eyes wide-open. The infinite, ah</u> 11:15:48—11 hours 23 minutes ago.

Lutavia arrived from Google on "NO HAY TAL LUGAR" 25/07/2010 by searching for <u>The nuclear horses still gallop among the rusted, inert machines, under the branches of the days, this spasm</u> 11:23:12—11 hours 31 minutes ago.

Lutavia arrived from Google on "NO HAY TAL LUGAR" 25/07/2010 by searching for <u>But autumn came—you know?—and I will proceed among the excessively tall sprigs with this shield and with this scepter</u> 11:30:23—11 hours 38 minutes ago.

The place of origin and the arrival path never varied. Lutavia. Google. By searching for. But the long, underlined messages continued to appear all summer and even into the fall without providing any other kind of information or favoring another approach. It was on an afternoon in September that I decided to copy the lines and paste them in a document, which I saved as "Lutavia Stops" (the title I had given to the little text on the subject I published on Tuesday, March 30, 2004 at 8:38AM). By then I had read about the already strange activities of that solitary, almost always naked man who inhabited, as far as I understood, the zones most affected by the radiation. The lines my feedjit captured also suggested that he spent his days among fiercely galloping horses, plants in colors increasingly unrecognizable to the human eye, sheets of onion paper, and rusted remains of hundreds of thousands of war tanks. He frequently referenced the peculiar sound of the echo that emerged from banging the tank's shell with a horse femur, for example. He also frequently described his way of floating along with the current of a river that he insisted on calling Pripyat.

Lutavia arrived from Google on "NO HAY TAL LUGAR" 09/09/2010 by searching for It has to do with stretching your muscles and letting yourself go. It has to do with opening your eyes and your hands and your skin and your fingernails. This is the water that beholds 11:36:19—10 hours 43 minutes ago.

His visits became quite frequent at the beginning of November and, as a result, I was able to compose a brief text about a primitive man who prepared for the winter cold with a couple of books, two radio programs, a cowhide, a partially handmade computer, and a lot of dedication. Instead of repeating what I had been doing up until then, which was to copy and paste his lines in my digital file, I opted to type out the phrases one by one on those old receipts that secretaries once used to record telephone messages (3x6 cm rectangles). Once I finished this task, and without thinking it all the way through, I sewed them together on their left-hand side.

My little book of you. The messages from November helped me produce six of these little volumes. With the December visits I made fifteen more. Forms of writing are quite varied.

Lutavia arrived from Google on "NO HAY TAL LUGAR" 30/12/2010 by searching for "I hoped everything would stay behind. Erased or crossed out forever. I hoped. But nothing, not even the bird, vanished." I am about to weigh anchor 11:48:33—9 hours 07 minutes ago.

I was afraid he might get too close, it's true. The shock. The capsizing right at my stomach's opening. I was afraid, upon reading the phrases in the feedjit, that he was already dead. Weighing anchor is so close to anchoring and vice versa. I opened the box where I had stored the little books composed of his phrases. I touched them. I flipped through some. Then I closed the box again. I thought many times that, upon hearing the knocking on the wooden door, I would have to take my few belongings and flee. This is the tongue click. And this is the smile with which you say: maybe later. I immediately calmed down when I repeated "nothing is real." And I calmed down even more when I took into consideration that, in the case that all this was real, the man was far away. Lutavia. Then I took a long, slow breath and stood up from the desk where my laptop rested and nibbled on things: chunks of bread, cheese rinds, potato peels. Then I even washed my hair.

Lutavia arrived from Google on "NO HAY TAL LUGAR" 21/03/2010 by searching for This is the moment you dream about a moose. Now the horses pass over the steppe, illuminated. Look, here. On this line. This is the moment you wake up 21/03/2010 11:27:12—10 hours 21 minutes ago.

Publication Notes

The pieces in this collection were translated from the Spanish by Sarah Booker unless otherwise noted at the end of an individual story. Additionally, each story appears here for the first time in English translation unless specified in the notes below.

NOSTALGIA. First English translation by Lisa Dillman in *Best of Contemporary Mexican Fiction*, Dalkey Archive Press, 2009.

AUTOETHNOGRAPHY WITH THE OTHER. First English translation by Francisca González Arias in *Literal*, 2014.

CARPATHIAN MOUNTAIN WOMAN. First English translation by Alex Ross in *BOMB*, 2012.

SIMPLE PLEASURE. PURE PLEASURE. First English translation by Sarah Booker in *The Paris Review*, 2018.

SPÍ UÑIEEY MAT. First English translation by Sarah Booker in *Latin American Literature Today*, 2017.

THE DATE. First English translation by Sarah Booker in *iMex*, 2018.

Author, translator, and critic CRISTINA RIVERA GARZA's recent publications include *Autobiografía del algodón*; *Grieving: Dispatches from a Wounded Country*, translated by Sarah Booker; *The Restless Dead: Necrowriting and Disappropriation*, translated by Robin Myers; and *La Castañeda Insane Asylum: Narratives of Pain from Modern Mexico*, translated by Laura Kanost. She is Distinguished Professor and founder of the PhD Program in Creative Writing in Spanish at the University of Houston, Department of Hispanic Studies. In 2018, Dorothy published her novel *The Taiga Syndrome*, translated by Aviva Kana and Suzanne Jill Levine. In 2020, Rivera Garza was named a MacArthur Fellow in Fiction.

SARAH BOOKER is a literary translator and doctoral candidate in Hispanic Literature at the University of North Carolina Chapel Hill, where she studies contemporary Latin American narrative and translation studies. Her translations include Cristina Rivera Garza's *The Iliac Crest* and *Grieving: Dispatches from a Wounded Country* and Mónica Ojeda's *Jawbone*.

LISA DILLMAN translates primarily Spanish-language fiction and teaches at Emory University. She has won numerous awards for her work, including the Best Translated Book Award and the Oxford-Weidenfeld Translation Prize, and has been a National Book Award Finalist in Translated Literature.

FRANCISCA GONZÁLEZ ARIAS is a professor of Spanish and a translator. In addition to English translations of Cristina Rivera

Garza, Soledad Puértolas, and Emilia Pardo Bazán, she has also published Spanish translations of poems by Emily Dickinson.

ALEX ROSS's published translations include short fiction by Mexican author Felipe Garrido and numerous books on art. His translation of Roberto Arlt's play *La Isla Desierta* (*The Desert Isle*) won first prize at the 2009 Midwest Translation Festival in St. Paul, Minnesota, where it was performed. He lives in Brooklyn.

DOROTHY, A PUBLISHING PROJECT

DOROTHYPROJECT.COM